Family Album

by
Claribel Alegría

translated by
Amanda Hopkinson

CURBSTONE PRESS

FIRST EDITION, 1991
Copyright © 1991 by Claribel Alegría
Translation Copyright © 1990
by Amanda Hopkinson
ALL RIGHTS RESERVED

El Detén (*The Talisman*) copyright © Claribel Alegría 1977, first
published by Editorial Lumen, Barcelona, 1977. *Album Familiar*
(*Family Album*) © Claribel Alegría 1982, first published by
EDUCA, San José, Costa Rica, 1982. *Pueblo de dios y de Mandinga*
(*Village of God and the Devil*) copyright © Claribel Alegría 1985,
first published by Ediciones Era SA, Mexico, 1985.
This collection first published as *Pueblo de Dios y de Mandinga*
by Editorial Lumen, Barcelona, 1986.
Family Album first published in English by Women's Press LTD,
1990, a member of the Namara Group, 34 Sutton Place, London,
ECIV 0DX.

The translation for the U.S. edition has been adapted slightly by
Curbstone editors to conform with American English. Special
thanks to Darwin J. Flakoll for his editorial help.

This publication was supported in part by donations, and by
a grant from The Connecticut Commission on the Arts, a state
agency whose funds are recommended by the Governor and
appropriated by the State Legislature.

Front cover graphic by Naúl Ojeda
Cover design by Stone Graphics
Printed in the U.S. by BookCrafters

Cloth edition ISBN: 0-915306-72-2
Paperback edition ISBN: 0-915306-94-8
Library of Congress number: 91-55413

distributed by
InBook
Box 120470
East Haven, CT 06512

published by
CURBSTONE PRESS
321 Jackson Street
Willimantic, CT 06226

CONTENTS

FAMILY ALBUM

The Talisman

"It's so boring, Mr. Magoo," said Karen pensively.

"It's better than Key West," said Mr. Magoo with the hint of a shrug.

"No," protested Karen. "The weekends are unbearable. Every Friday at six o'clock precisely Daddy arrives to pick me up at the school entrance and take me home. Then I help him make dinner, we watch television, play cards and on Saturday and Sunday afternoons I have to stay at home alone while he goes to play golf with his friends."

"What?" Mr. Magoo cut in, "golf and not tennis?"

"And at home there's nothing to do. No records, books, nothing. The most gripping book he's got is about techniques for selling real estate. I'm not even allowed a pet cat."

"Come off it," said Mr. Magoo, whose real name was Fritz Fitzpatrick and who lived in Key West. He played tennis with Miss Muffet and Miss Muffet always won, for in spite of his thick glasses in their tortoise-shell frames Mr. Magoo either couldn't see the ball or saw three balls at once. "Don't exaggerate, sweetheart, and try to make some friends. I'm sure there must be at least a few friendly girls on the block."

"No, not one," Karen answered impatiently. "The only one I took to was Lily, but Daddy stopped me going around with her because her parents let her run wild and smoke dope."

"Your father was right."

"Lily says that dope doesn't harm you, it only makes you want to laugh a lot and see flowers with faces and hear colors talking and . . ."

Mr. Magoo wagged his index finger to show he was about to say something very important, but Karen heard footsteps approaching and quickly said goodbye.

"Hello, Susan," she said, smoothing her navy pleated skirt.

"The Reverend Mother wants to see you," said Susan self-importantly.

"Me?" asked Karen, startled. "I don't remember having done anything wrong."

"She says you should go at once to her office and that she wants to talk to you."

Whatever does the old girl want? wondered Karen, as she skirted the fountain in the middle of the courtyard. I couldn't care less . . . oh well perhaps (she could feel her stomach fluttering a little) — no, no I'm really not bothered. What will Daddy make of it though? Does it really matter? What he'll do is give one of his little coughs, he always finds it hard to get started, and say: "I don't know what to do with you, Karen." That'll leave me feeling so embarrassed, because he'll be on the verge of tears and it's true, he hasn't a clue what to do.

Karen tapped on the door with her knuckles.

"Come in," replied a stern voice.

Controlling her impulse to run away, Karen regained her self-possession and went into a room that smelled of beeswax candles and worm-eaten statues.

"Sit down," said the Reverend Mother, peering at her over her spectacles.

Karen sat down on the black plastic chair facing her.

The Reverend Mother removed her gold-rimmed spectacles and placed them on the glass surface of her broad mahogany desk, then rubbed her eyes.

"You know why I've sent for you, don't you?"

Karen shook her head.

"But you ought to know," said the nun, replacing her spectacles.

Again Karen experienced a terrible urge to run away, but clung to the edge of her chair and waited.

"This is a report on your behavior," explained the Reverend Mother picking up a typewritten sheet of paper on her right. "The Sister who produced it complains" — she brandished the paper under Karen's nose before replacing it on the desk — "that you don't do your homework, you don't pay attention, you spend all your time daydreaming and distracting your fellow pupils. What do you have to say for yourself?"

Karen said nothing.

"It's not a matter of playing dumb, my dear. If you want to stay here with us, you must learn to recognize your faults and try to correct them."

Karen remained stubbornly silent.

"Can you imagine the problems your father would be faced with if we decided to expel you?"

The sudden mention of the word "expel" made the girl tremble.

"Don't be afraid, it won't come to that. At least as far as this year is concerned, I want to see you settle in with us. I've promised your father that we'll try to help you, but you'll have to pull your weight as well. Will you promise me to do that?"

Karen said nothing. From where she was sitting she could see the acacia tree in the opposite garden. All Nicolasa's birds had flown out of their cages and the tree was filled with colors.

"What's the matter? Are you feeling ill?"

Karen clenched her fists to control the trembling that had seized her, and shook her head.

"You're an intelligent young woman, and it's not too much to ask that you make a little more effort in class for Our Lord's sake, He who suffered so much for ours. You're not a child any more, after all. How old are you?"

"Fifteen."

"It isn't right for you to be so scatterbrained. You should be capable of concentrating harder and achieving more by now. What's going on in that little head of yours? The world isn't a fairy tale, and you have to learn to come to terms with it."

A heavy and prolonged silence followed, and suddenly Karen noticed that the acacia tree had shed its birds.

The Reverend Mother sighed.

"Why do you insist on making things so difficult for me? Perhaps you need a spiritual director, someone in whom you can confide. Do you like the idea? You could choose one for yourself."

Another silence.

"Perhaps you'd consider Sister Petronella, as she's also Latin American?"

Karen shook her head. No.

"Well, then you suggest someone."

Karen was lost in thought for a few moments as she mentally reviewed the faces of her teachers. She had succeeded in overcoming her shivers and again felt mistress of herself.

"Sister Mary Ann," she at last concluded aloud, a note of triumph in her voice.

"Pardon?" The Reverend Mother was shocked.

"Definitely," said Karen, having just sworn to herself that it could only be her: Sister Mary Anne, the dragon, her chief persecutor, the one who must have written that report, with her eyes as sharp as broken glass and a voice like a flute out of tune.

"As you wish," replied the nun with a hint of impatience, "but think it over carefully. I'll give you until Thursday to decide."

That night Karen couldn't sleep. She tossed and turned in her bed, counting sheep with her eyes tightly closed. No luck. Images and voices broke through the darkness, danced before her, drawing nearer, enlarging themselves until they acquired hallucinatory dimensions. There was Mark, obliging her to serve as his model, his orange motorbike speeding through the streets of Key West while she clung to his back, shrieking. Mark's voice, commanding her not to mention anything to her mother, her grandmother's voice yelling at Mark and her mother that they were mad, her grandfather's hoarse voice ordering Mark out of the house from the depths of his easy-chair, and again the orange motorbike, the sailing skiff in the harbor, Mark's interminable sentences and the eyes, her mother's eyes. She longed to scream. She covered her head with the blanket and began sobbing into her pillow. Mark went on talking and she was unable to stop him so she covered up her ears and banged her head against the pillow against the eyes, her mother's eyes.

Sister Mary Ann was sitting on a sort of dais at the far end of the room in her upright wicker-backed chair. She continued scrutinizing the papers covering her desk without pausing to look at the children entering the room.

I wonder what on earth Missouri is doing now? Karen asked herself. It's bound to be a lot more fun than what's going on here. "Karen," Sister Mary Ann suddenly interrupted, "I want you to repeat the lesson to me."

She leapt to her feet awkwardly and began stammering.

From the seat behind her, Susan attempted to help her out.

"Shhh," interrupted Sister Mary Ann, "come on, Karen."

"The Battle of Concord . . ." she began, attempting to draw out each syllable.

"Quite so," replied the nun, "when did it take place?"

She tried her hardest to concentrate and remember but the only date that came to mind was 1718, the year in which (according to Missouri), a terrible pirate called Blackbeard met his death, and what on earth did Blackbeard have to do with the Battle of Concord?

"Very well," said Sister Mary Ann with unaccustomed patience — clearly the Reverend Mother had already had words with her "if you can't remember that, then tell us what you can remember."

Karen began talking about "the Boston tea party," the only chapter she could bring to mind. Some of the girls began giggling, then she herself giggled, and an incredulous Sister Mary Ann had to put a finger to her lips.

"That's enough," she said, "sit down. Once again, I see, you have not done your homework."

So what's new? thought Karen.

Susan recited the lesson word-perfectly. All the nuns adored her. She spent all her free time studying and offering daily sacrifices. She kept a record on scraps of paper: "Today I didn't eat any pudding for love of Him. Today I told a lie and I

13

repent. I'll make my confession for certain this Wednesday." She had a crush on the catechism teacher who was very pretty with her blue eyes and marble-hued skin, and made no bones about admitting it.

"Karen," said Sister Mary Ann when the class was over, "I want to speak to you a moment."

She waited in silence at her desk until all the girls had filed out.

"Why didn't you do your homework?" asked the nun.

"I did study a little bit," she attempted to defend herself while wringing her hands, "but . . ."

"No buts. Remember how Our Lord doesn't appreciate our telling lies."

Our Lord, Our Lord, forever Our Lord. I'll bet he was as much of a liar as me if *you think you're so cool walk across my swimming pool,* I'll never swallow the bit about walking on the water without sinking.

"The Reverend Mother wants you and I to be at her office at six o'clock," the nun said, "but first you must write a single-page summary of today's lesson and bring it to me here. It's already four o'clock," she concluded, looking at her pocket watch, "so hurry up."

Karen nodded her head and made for the door.

"What do you say before leaving the room?" protested the nun, in the same rasping tones as before.

"Excuse me please," added Karen and continued running to her dormitory.

"The old witch" she muttered, retrieving the book of North American history from her closet, "and there I was thinking she might have improved."

She opened the book at the chapter on the Revolution and started reading. "Seventeen seventy-five. Of course. How on earth did I get it into my head that it was 1718?"

As she read and took notes in her exercise book she smelled a powerful scent of tamarind; in Los Angeles there were no tamarind trees.

She raised her voice to ask. "Is that you, Missouri? Leave me to finish this and then I'll join you."

But Missouri paid no attention and planted himself right in front of her, his face like a newly washed plate and his feet bare, peeling a tamarind.

Karen felt her mouth watering and her concentration wavering. "Hurry up," said Missouri, "and I'll tell you all about what happened to me on the coral reef."

"Wait a minute, this is really important."

"Don't be a bore," the boy began to get impatient.

"If you don't leave me alone I'll tell Nicolasa. I've got to finish this summary before six o'clock and I've no stomach for a spat with the Reverend Mother."

"Come on Karen, don't tell me that you've gone all silly," Missouri had an impish look. "How could what you're doing possibly be more important than climbing up the tamarind tree and eating and eating until your mouth turns sour, or swimming out to the coral reef and sitting there watching the waves making shadows on the bottom, and then diving deep down, frightening the octopi from their caves and throwing sand at the water snails, watching them spinning around and around without knowing where they're going?"

"Do you know," Karen asked, "in what year the Battle of Concord took place?"

"No," replied Missouri, "I only know that in 1718 Blackbeard was put to death for being a terribly wicked but wonderfully brave pirate and that what he did was worth ten Battles of Concord."

"What do you know about it?" Karen burst out laughing while attempting to concentrate on what she was doing.

"Let me tell you," insisted Missouri.

"My God you're stubborn. I've got to behave properly today. Hang on a minute."

Missouri waited quietly, staring down at his toes, but before Karen could finish he resumed the attack:

"After school I felt like going swimming."

Karen remembered the warm, green, translucent water caressing her body as she plunged through it, and tears almost sprang to her eyes.

"I was all out of breath when I reached the reef," said Missouri, turning cartwheels around the room, "so I sat down with my eyes shut because they were stinging from the salt, when suddenly I felt something move close beside me."

"A shark!" exclaimed Karen.

"Worse than that, one of those moray eels."

"How horrible. Did you have your knife?"

"No" replied Missouri, sinking down on the carpet in lotus position.

"You're crazy, your mother always told us that we should take a penknife when we went out to the reef."

"I know that," said Missouri disdainfully, "but I'd never seen a creature like that so I thought she'd made them up."

"He could have clamped his jaws down on you and not let go until you drowned."

"I was so scared that I didn't even have time to think. When I came to my senses I was half-way back to the beach and — do you know what?"

They heard voices approaching and Karen jumped and picked up her pencil again, as Missouri vanished leaving a pungent scent of tamarind behind him.

"Hi," said Susan, spilling an armload of books over the bed, "do you know what Sister Magdalena told me?"

"No. How could I?"

Susan sat herself down on the edge of the bed, removed her shoes and slid her feet into her slippers.

"They say that Sister Mary Ann has been really nervous lately, and that last night her hands were trembling as she picked up her spoon and she spilled soup all down her habit."

"What's that got to do with me?" Karen asked without stopping writing.

"It's *because* of you she's like that," Susan smiled. "It's because you've chosen her as your spiritual adviser. Sister Magdalena said that Sister Mary Ann, who's always been so aloof and bitter, approached her on some pretext or other last night and asked how spiritual daughters are supposed to be treated. It's the first time anyone has wanted to be close to her and she's terrified. Sister Magdalena says you're a weird girl who doesn't really know what she's doing."

"I'm not up to anything." Karen's eyes opened wide in innocence. "I thought if I chose the most embittered nun of the lot perhaps our blessed Reverend Mother would decide to leave me in peace. And I couldn't care less about spiritual advisers."

"It's obvious you're a newcomer and still don't understand how the establishment functions. As of now you and Sister Mary Ann will be spending a lot of time together."

"Well I think you're wrong. Sister Mary Ann's so antisocial she'll do her best to keep me at arm's length."

"You're the one who's wrong," Susan looked at her sadly. "She's very aware of her obligations and will try her hardest to straighten you out. Why didn't you pick Sister Magdalena? She's intelligent and gets on well with young people. I love talking to her."

"And what do you talk about?"

"I don't know, lots of things. She treats me as a friend. She even passes on bits of gossip. She says that she's sorry for Sister Mary Ann, who comes from a poorer background, and says all the nuns try to avoid her because she takes everything to heart and each time she says anything it comes out sounding too intense and over-dogmatic. She even sets the Reverend Mother on edge."

"I've definitely put my foot in it," Karen muttered to herself dispiritedly and resumed doodling on her exercise book.

"You're going to see the Reverend Mother today, aren't you?"

"Yes. How come you know?"

"Sister Magdalena told me." Susan smiled and went over to her desk.

"Sit down a minute," said Karen's father as soon as they got in from school.

Karen took off her raincoat, put her bookbag on the table in the middle of the room and sat down in the armchair facing the fireplace.

"Reverend Mother phoned me yesterday." Her father wiped his forehead with a monogrammed linen handkerchief. "She said that things aren't going well with your studies. What do you think?"

"If what they taught were more interesting I promise you I'd be studying."

"Stop being silly and let's talk like two reasonable human beings."

Karen suddenly found herself fixated on the square fireplace. What's going to happen now? she wondered. Who's going to appear out of this enormous black mouth?

"Are you happy here?" her father asked.

"Yes, but I'd rather not have to go to school."

"And stay uneducated?" He began to grow impatient. "I still haven't fathomed how your mother allowed you to go a whole year without school."

"Mark says that schools are useless, that you can learn a lot more observing snails and plants and insects."

"I've never heard such rubbish," his voice rose as he interrupted her. "I'll never forgive your mother for having left you in the hands of that idiot. I'm not sure if you realize what I went through when they took you off without a word to me. Six years without hearing anything and suddenly *voila* — here's *your* daughter for you to look after."

"Would you have preferred never to see me again?"

"Don't be stupid. But such things just aren't done and I think you ought to know as much. What did Mark have to say about me?"

"Nothing. Only that you were a good sort."

"Nothing else?"

"You won't be offended?"

"No." His hand was trembling slightly as he opened a cigarette packet.

"That you lack imagination."

"And what else?"

Karen returned her gaze to the fireplace and there stood Nicolasa: *Be patient, honey, he only wants what's best for you.*

She hardly had time to smile at her when her father's voice interrupted:

"What are you laughing at?"

"Nothing."

"At me, isn't it?"

"How could you think such a thing? I promise I'm not," said Karen. She looked back at the square fireplace.

There's no sense in repeating what you hear at home, said Nicolasa.

"What else did he tell you?" It was her father's voice again and Karen jumped.

"I don't know, he hardly ever mentioned you."

She looked again at the fireplace and Nicolasa waved goodbye with a smile.

Don't go, Karen pleaded silently, I want to talk to you.

"Why do you keep staring at the fireplace?" her father asked. "You never used to be so distracted and it's not right. What did you do with your time while all the other children were at school?"

Karen had a great urge to recount all the many things she had learned: remedies for the evil eye, for black widow spiders and snake bites, all those things Nicolasa taught them and nobody else knew, but she limited herself to a shrug of the shoulders.

"Come on, tell," he insisted.

"I learned how to swim a bit, and to distinguish poisonous plants and disease-carrying insects. At night Mark would teach me the names of the stars."

"And your mother never thought of giving you a book to read?"

"But of course," she said with enthusiasm. "I read *El Quijote*, the whole of Jules Verne and . . ."

"I meant school texts." He had become irritated.

Karen shook her head. Mark used to say that they were useless.

"Unbelievable." He exhaled the smoke through his nostrils. "Tomorrow I must write to Natalia and request the reports done at your last school, the Reverend Mother needs them in order to know how to place you in class. She's a remarkable woman."

"But Daddy!" Karen exclaimed.

"You ought to know," he interrupted, "that the nuns did me a great favour by taking you in without any kind of grades, without proof you'd ever attended school. All I'm asking is that you try and co-operate with your teachers a little, do you promise me this much?"

"Yes," she heard herself say in a cavernous voice. Her eyes returned to the fireplace. Nicolasa had disappeared.

"Right, you can be off now. Tonight we'll be eating out with friends."

Karen felt a sudden impulse to hug and kiss her father, and threw herself on to his lap, putting her arms about his neck.

"What's up?" he asked in surprise, starting back.

"Nothing, I just love you a lot and promise to study and not be distracted," she said, giving him a kiss.

"Fine, fine," he pushed her aside gently. "We'll see what happens. Now hurry and get yourself dressed, we've got to go out in half an hour."

"Surprised to see me?" asked Mark, appearing as Karen was undressing and thinking how tedious the evening's social gathering had been. "I saw you were getting very bored so I came back."

"Who told you I was bored?" asked Karen, rummaging in her chest of drawers.

"What are you looking for?"

"My talisman. Missouri gave it to me and now I've lost it."

"Oh but that's serious. You should never lose a talisman, it brings bad luck."

"I know." She resumed her desperate search. "Maybe I left it at school."

"Your school must be pretty boring."

"You're wrong. There are some really friendly girls and all the teachers like me a lot."

"Remember I'm the one you can't deceive." Mark drew closer, looking deep into her eyes. "It's fine for you to lie to your father or to the Reverend Mother or your spiritual adviser" — he burst out laughing — "but remember not to try it on me."

Karen felt a shiver run over her body.

"All right," she admitted, "I do sometimes get bored."

"I knew I wasn't mistaken," Mark shook his index finger at her. "And your father also bores you, doesn't he?"

"That's not true," said Karen, getting into bed. "I'm happy to be with him."

"Come on now, don't lie," Mark sat himself down on the edge of her bed.

Karen noticed he was smelling strongly of alcohol.

"You've been drinking?"

"What if I have?" he said, narrowing his eyes. "Your father's a drag, isn't he?"

"He's good and helps as much as he can but yes, you're right, I do get a bit fed up."

"Nobody to tell you stories, right?" He came still closer.

"No," whispered Karen, pulling the sheet right up to her neck. "How's Mommy?"

"She also likes my stories."

"You're nuts," said Karen, and felt herself flush.

"Once upon a time there was a spider." ·

"No, please not now," interrupted Karen. "How's Bolita?"

"Or would you rather have the centipede?"

"Go away and don't come back." She covered her face with the sheet.

"Okay, okay," he said with a malicious smirk, "how nervous you are today."

Karen waited for a few minutes with her face covered then, little by little, she lowered the sheets. Mark had disappeared. She began to cry softly until sleep overwhelmed her.

The clock had just struck seven and Karen hurriedly scrabbled for her mantilla in the drawer. Once again she'd be late for chapel.

"Karen," Natalia was flapping a sheet of paper in her hand, "what did you say to your father to make him write me such a stupid letter? Remember, before sending you to him we talked on several occasions, and you promised never to complain about my life with Mark. Now see what you've done" — she was shaking the letter violently — "I'd never have thought you capable of such a thing."

Karen retreated in fear until her back was up against the wall. She pressed heavily against it.

"It was Daddy who started questioning me," she vacillated, "and I couldn't lie to him. The Reverend Mother needed to know so she could place me in class."

"You're a little fool," Natalia was harsh, "you could've made up something."

"I'm fed up with lies." Karen's indignation helped her recover her self-possession. "And any time Daddy asks me something I mean to tell him the truth. He doesn't approve of your not sending me to school for a whole year. If you don't like it, why don't you save your sermons for Mark rather than coming and pestering me?"

"You're turning out impossible," said Natalia dryly.

"And Daddy also wants to know what went on in Guatemala," Karen broke in. "Perhaps I should tell him about that. How old was I then? Ten?"

"With your vivid imagination, no doubt you've exaggerated everything out of all proportion."

"That would be difficult. The worst part is that you knew perfectly well before even taking us there that Grandfather was recuperating from a heart attack."

"He was almost well again," Natalia raised her voice, "the heart attack that killed him happened when we were in Key West, barely two years ago. Don't you remember how he spent the whole time in his rocking chair? If it hadn't been for that clown Eduardo, he'd never have noticed."

"Of course he would, with Mark shouting so loudly you could hear him from the garage about how bored he was with that stupid village and its moronic inhabitants."

"Grandfather was almost deaf," Natalia made an impatient gesture.

"But Grandmother wasn't, nor were any of the people who came to visit them."

"Hardly anyone came."

"That was your fault as well." Karen pushed herself upright with her shoulder. She clasped her hands and automatically made as if to wash them. "Any time someone came you behaved as hatefully as possible. So what would you think" — she stared accusingly at her mother — "if I told Daddy about the dog in the rain?"

"What dog?"

"Oh, I thought you had a better memory than that. Don't you remember the story about the pistols either? What can you tell me about your Wild West act or have you forgotten that the whole family was involved in getting the two of you out of jail? How do you think Daddy would react to all that?"

"I'm fed up with these threats about your father. You can tell him what you like. I've long stopped caring what he thinks."

"The only good thing you ever did for me," Karen advanced on her mother, "was to send me here, far from that insane and unhealthy place. Shooting into the air from a car going full speed just for the hell of it — some joke!"

"Mark was ill," Natalia was trying to control the trembling of her lips, "and you're right, he was drinking too much, getting utterly bored in Guatemala. For once he wanted to get out of the trap he was in just for an evening and show me what a crack shot with a pistol he was."

"And why didn't he pick somewhere quieter?"

"We were on our way to the river." Natalia had recovered her composure. "We were taking bottles and empty tins to use as targets. The trouble was that he insisted on driving. He took a wrong turn and we ended up in a one-way street and when he heard the police whistle Mark got furious and reacted by firing into the air. It was a childish prank, if you like, but nothing like as terrible as my family painted it, just a puerile act of defiance."

"They didn't take it like that down at the police station." Karen's hands made jerky movements as she approached her mother.

"Calm down." Natalia sounded worried.

"Nor did the judge," continued Karen, paying no attention, "and that really disgusted Grandfather. How much did Mark's little adventure cost him in fines?"

Natalia didn't reply and Karen kept advancing until she suddenly noticed her mother had disappeared and she was left making threatening gestures at the door and furiously muttering, "Damn, damn, damn!"

"Why weren't you at Vespers last night?" demanded Sister Mary Ann, without raising her eyes from her crocheting.

"I was feeling ill," lied Karen, "and slept through."

"All right, then," sighed the nun, "sit down. This is our eighth session and we don't seem to have made any progress at all. Why don't you tell me more about yourself? I can see you're unhappy in school, that you'd prefer to run around barefoot and spend all day on the beach, but I don't really know anything else. Tell me something about your mother, she is bound to be worried about you."

"Yes," admitted Karen, "she does worry. The night I ran away with Missouri she and Mark went out on the motorbike and searched everywhere and when at last they found me in Missouri's garden Mommy hugged me tight and burst into tears."

"And what were you doing there at night?" asked the nun.

"Nothing. We were watching a fiesta, but it wasn't a fiesta for children," she added in a mysterious voice, "and nobody realized we were spying on them."

"I don't understand. Explain yourself. What kind of a fiesta?"

"A lot of people were there, and all of them were black."

"And your mother allowed you to mix with them?"

"Why not?" she feigned surprise.

"There are certain limits one ought to observe," replied the nun, straightening herself in her chair, "you'll understand such things better in due course. Continue."

"We'd climbed up into a guava tree so we couldn't see very well."

"Tell me all you remember, don't be afraid."

"There were lots of chairs scattered around and an altar at the end of the room."

"I beg your pardon?" Sister Mary Ann's eyes widened. "They were celebrating Mass?"

"Yes." Karen began to warm to her subject, a shiver of delight in her stomach. How amusing to observe the old woman growing scandalized over nothing! "The celebrant was Missouri's uncle, Mr. Sherbert's brother. Everyone was dancing and singing, and Mr. Sherbert joined in, and some men standing close to him were playing tambourines and singing in beautiful voices. Two other men were holding up a poor squealing lamb by the hooves."

"A Black Mass!" gasped Sister Mary Ann. "Go on, go on."

"They also had a chicken that Mr. Sherbert's brother began to swing around in the air. The feathers drifted down and the lamb went on bleating while the singing and banging of tambourines got louder and louder and finally they wrung the chicken's neck and lots of blood spurted out."

"Savages!" exclaimed the nun. "Why didn't your mother forbid such friendships?"

"And Nicolasa got up from her chair," Karen was quite carried away, "and began to dance. Her flesh quivered and everyone stared at her and she suddenly fell to the floor. That frightened me dreadfully, but Missouri said not to worry, it always happened. Then everyone began dancing around Nicolasa and that was when they slit the goat's throat."

"Savages!" repeated the nun. Her eyes narrowed and her lips developed a strange downward twist.

"And they anointed her face with the blood," Karen went on, "and Mr. Sherbert's too. Then it was all over. Afterwards they went on singing and dancing and other women fell to the floor, all crying out and with their flesh shaking like Nicolasa's. Missouri says that back in Haiti his mother was queen of this dancing, but that it's not a dance, it's a religion."

"Possessed by the devil!" pronounced Sister Mary Ann, removing the pins and placing the fabric on her lap. "Don't you realize, child, the good fortune you've had to escape from such an inferno? Does your father know all this?"

"No. I've never told him any of it."

"But you ought to have."

"No, otherwise he'll start going on about Mommy and Mark to me, and I love them a lot. Mark used to tell me pretty stories."

"Right," said Sister Mary Ann. "That's enough for one day. Have you done your homework?"

"Yes," replied Karen, taking three notebooks out of her bookbag, and thinking, How stupid I am for not having scandalized her sooner! She's a funny old thing.

Sister Mary Ann carefully examined the notebooks.

"Fine," she concluded after a minute's perusal, "this time you've worked harder. Your reward will be to come to the garden with me tomorrow and cut flowers for the chapel. Would you like that?"

"I would. And I'd also like to hear about when you were a child."

"We'll talk about that later. Now run along. No, wait a moment," she added, intercepting Karen at the door. "Has Susan ever told you anything bad that Sister Magdalena said about me?"

"No," lied Karen. "She hasn't mentioned anything."

"All right, all right," muttered the nun, her face burning. "You can go now."

"You see how pleased Sister Mary Ann is with you for doing your homework?" asked Karen's grandmother, hugging her tenderly.

"No, Grandma, you're mistaken there. What she likes is being told stories."

"She's a good woman and loves you dearly," replied the grandmother, shaking her newly washed hair that reached nearly to her waist.

"Wrong again," interrupted Karen. "If you heard how she criticizes all the other nuns, especially Sister Magdalena, just because she's young and pretty and all the girls love her. She says she doesn't have a true vocation, that she became a nun because her boyfriend left her for someone else, and that she's a vain creature who doesn't know how to do anything."

"We're all human, child," Grandmother burst out laughing. "Try to be a little more patient."

"Has Mommy written to you?"

"No," Grandmother sighed. "Natalia never writes. I'd be surprised if she'd done more than send a postcard ever since you came. My poor child, she's hypnotized by that man."

"Mark's all right," Karen said defensively, "and he's very charming. It's only when he's drunk that he loses his head."

"Don't talk rubbish." Her grandmother was becoming excited. "If there's one thing I'm pleased about it's that Natalia finally came to her senses and removed you from those horrible surroundings."

"See how irritable you are as well? But you smell delicious, I can't work out if it's gardenia or citrus blossom," said Karen, closing her eyes. "How I'd love to return to the old farm and eat *salpores* and cashews and *chilate* with dumplings and lots of honey."

"You're gorgeous and I adore you," said Grandmother, hugging her again. "If you only knew how I miss you. Maybe your father will send you to spend a holiday with me, would you like me to ask him when there's a moment?"

Karen nodded.

"And has Natalia written to you?"

"Hardly at all. Do you think she misses me?"

"Of course, my love, it must have been a terrible sacrifice to tear herself away from you, and even if she doesn't write to you, you must write to her."

"I think Mark must be drinking again."

"Why do you think that? Has Natalia mentioned anything?"

"No, it's just a feeling. And I'm happy to be here."

Grandmother hugged her to her bosom, kissed her on the forehead and receded, making the sign of the cross.

"What sort of stories did Mark tell you?" inquired Sister Mary Ann while they were cutting roses for the chapel.

"Loads of them, but those that frightened me most were the ones about the spider and the centipede."

"Explain what you mean. What was the one about the spider?"

"It'll scare you too." Karen broke into silent laughter.

"Begin now, don't be bashful."

Bashful my foot!

"Once upon a time there was a spider. No, perhaps better not. Why don't you tell me something about yourself first?"

"What do you want me to tell you?"

"Where you were born, why you became a nun, what your parents were like."

"What a curious girl you are." The nun raised her hands in mild exasperation.

And you, what an idiot, thought Karen.

"Right, but promise me that afterwards you'll tell me the story about the spider?"

"I promise."

"Take the scissors and cut some yellow roses, they'll shine on their long stems. Really, there's not a lot to tell you. I was born in New Orleans, but my parents came from Ireland."

"Hello," called Susan from the corridor, "having fun?"

"Lots," Karen laughed, and then returned to the nun. "One of Mommy's grandfathers also came over from Ireland. Was your father a drunk?"

"What are you saying?" The nun's cheeks were again beginning to flame. "My parents were respectable people."

"Mommy says that all Irish are drunkards but are very charming and sing beautifully."

"My parents were devout Christians and of extremely chaste habits," pronounced the nun, accenting *extremely*. "My father died from an ulcer when I was hardly thirteen, and my older brother was eighteen. My saintly mother, may Our Lord cherish her in His bosom, took care of our education."

"Did you have lots of brothers and sisters?"

"Oh my, yes." Sister Mary Ann again raised her arms heavenwards. "There are seven of us, three older and three younger than me."

"I would have liked a brother."

"Enough," said Sister Mary Ann, "don't cut any more roses, we've got plenty. Leave them on the flowerbed and water the pansies."

While Karen filled the watering can at the fountain, the nun continued talking as though to herself.

"We were a lovely family, every evening we recited the rosary together."

"Didn't you get bored?"

"How could you think such a thing!" The nun took a handkerchief out of her bag and wiped her eyes. "Did your mother never teach you to recite the rosary?"

"No," replied Karen, "Mark and Mommy are atheists. Aargh!" she exclaimed, suddenly jumping backwards.

"What happened?"

"There's a toad in the flowerbed."

"Why so shocked?" asked Sister Mary Ann, setting the flowers down. "They too are God's creatures."

She slowly approached the little animal who gazed at her in terror, and scooped it up in her hands.

"Come closer, have you ever looked at their eyes?"

"No," Karen shuddered with disgust.

"Come closer," insisted the nun, "look how beautiful they are, do you see the golden glints in their irises?"

The bell rang out calling the girls to their lessons, and a horde of children swarmed through the corridors.

"Hurry along," said Sister Mary Ann, "you mustn't be late on my account."

She replaced the little creature on the ground with great tenderness, and joined the girls going into the chapel.

Yes, it was Miss Muffet, without a doubt. She'd emerged from a patch of damp on the wall, and there she was very straight and very thin, looking at Karen over the top of her gold-rimmed glasses.

"Little Miss Muffet
sat on a tuffet
eating her curds and whey,"

Karen sang in a low voice and Miss Muffet, miracle of miracles, didn't shriek back as she had in Key West. Maybe she hasn't heard me, Karen thought and continued in a slightly louder voice:

"Along came a spider
and sat down beside her
and frightened Miss Muffet away."

"Always the same," said Miss Muffet in her soft voice, and the outline of a smile appeared etched in her dry, seamed cheeks.

"Miss Muffet!" Karen started. "I thought you'd never come."

"Why not? At heart you know I like you, you're all right."

Poor thing, thought Karen, it must be very sad to be a spinster. Miss Muffet, whose real name was Miss Robinson, lived alone in Key West at number 18. Her only friend was Mr. Magoo, who lived at number 23 and who also lived alone. Each afternoon they played tennis and Miss Muffet returned home very erect and serious, practicing strokes in the air with her racquet. Then she watered her flowers, and had tea and toast and little cakes stuffed with currants and spread with blackberry jam. Any time Karen and Missouri were in the vicinity she invited them in and offered them each a cake.

"How's Mr. Magoo?"

"Well. Walled up in his carpentry workshop and casting horoscopes."

Karen shut her eyes tightly and saw the room filled with tools and rare wood Mr. Magoo had imported from Lebanon, Peru and many other places, because when he was young Mr. Magoo had been a sailor and travelled everywhere and learned to play the lute. He taught Karen all the capitals of the world, and which was the highest mountain and who was the first person to scale it and a thousand other equally interesting facts.

Miss Muffet was still there when Karen opened her eyes.

"Why don't you marry him?" she asked Miss Muffet, who blushed and said nothing.

She's even uglier than Sister Mary Ann, thought Karen. Ugly as sin, her mother used to say, referring to Miss Muffet.

"It'd be more fun than living alone," Karen insisted.

"Don't be silly," Miss Muffet replied. "I'd never surrender my freedom to a man."

It wouldn't be fair to Mr. Magoo, thought Karen, he likes pretty girls too much. I wonder why she's come?

"To talk about Bolita," Miss Muffet read her thoughts.

Karen shifted uncomfortably in her chair.

"Is that your dog?" Miss Muffet had asked her the first time she and Missouri arrived with Bolita.

"Yes," answered Karen, "Miss Adams went to Europe and left her with Mommy."

"Incredible, incredible," murmured Miss Muffet without visible change in the insipid expression on her face.

"Why doesn't she ever laugh?" Karen had once asked Mr. Magoo.

"Because she's English," he'd replied.

"Why on earth did your mother take in a stray dog," Miss Muffet clicked her innumerable teeth, "when she can't even cope with feeding you a decent meal?"

Karen could feel tears pricking her eyelids but wouldn't permit herself more than a shrug of the shoulders. From that day on Miss Muffet never again invited them to come and eat cakes with currants and had eyes only for Bolita. Every afternoon she brought her into the kitchen and opened the door to the refrigerator that was always full. She purred as she brought out a piece of meat and served it up to the bitch in a black plastic dish. Once Missouri had asked her if she didn't have any more cakes like those she used to offer them and she had paused, staring at them with faded eyes, and told them that that's what their mothers were for. Karen and Missouri had left at a run with Bolita trotting behind, and Nicolasa had planted a kiss on their cheeks with her fresh lips and told them to pay no attention. She invited them to come and eat ices with meringue, which were altogether tastier than any cakes that Miss Muffet could provide.

"What about Bolita?" asked Karen.

"Yes," said Miss Muffet, "Mark kicked her the other day and left her wounded. I reported it to the Society for the Protection of Animals and if he dares to do such a thing again, I'm prepared to report him to the police. Since Bolita is your dog" — she added in a softer voice — "I thought you might agree to write to your mother and request that she give her to me. I promise I'd look after her carefully."

Karen remained silent. She thought it was better that way. Mark unemployed, aggressive, drinking, doubtless-drawing checks he couldn't back, preparing to run off again.

"Doesn't the idea appeal to you?" whispered Miss Muffet.

"Yes, yes," Karen hastened to reply, "I'll write tomorrow. Bolita would be fine with you."

"Thank you, darling," Miss Muffett stroked Karen's hair with her bony hand and vanished.

"Incredible, incredible," murmured Karen.

"So growing up in an atheist home, how did you come to make your first communion?" asked Sister Mary Ann, taking her crochet from its canvas bag. She was making an altar cloth for the Lady Chapel, and by now it was nearly finished.

"Grandmother insisted. I made it secretly because had Mark known about it he would have been furious. But this is the first time I've attended a Catholic school."

"And you're bored, aren't you?"

"A bit."

"How long did you live with Mark and your mother?"

"I'm not sure, I think about seven years."

"Seven years of immorality," whispered the nun.

"I beg your pardon?"

"Nothing, nothing," muttered the nun, concentrating on her needles, "now let's see, how about the spider story?"

"You still haven't told me anything about your life," protested the girl.

"What else do you want to know?"

"Lots of things. Like what the house was like where you used to live, if you went to the beach, if you had friends."

"I didn't need friends. As I explained, I had six brothers and sisters: altogether we were three boys and four girls. My mother raised us all according to God's laws." She raised her eyes.

Karen repressed a laugh. Every time Sister Mary Ann brought up sacred matters she rolled her eyes and twisted her neck around to the left.

"What do you find so amusing?" The nun looked at her sharply.

"Nothing, nothing," protested Karen. "How could you think such a thing? Where are your brothers and sisters now?"

"My two oldest brothers are priests," said the nun, returning to her handiwork. "One stayed in New Orleans and the other became a missionary in Peru. The youngest got married and has a fine Christian family."

"And your sisters?"

"All of us nuns, except one, the best. She sacrificed her life to caring for our mother until she passed away."

They must be all as ugly as her, and couldn't be anything but nuns or stay home to look after the old woman. She must've been a real dragon, thought Karen. She tried to compare her with her own grandmother, but her own grandmother was not a dragon, nor had she made Karen recite the rosary.

"What are you thinking about?"

"About my grandmother."

"One day you must tell me about her. According to your father she's a good woman, and very devout."

Karen nodded.

"Do you love her a lot?"

"Almost as much as my mother. I used to spend my holidays with her, but I haven't seen her since my grandfather died, over two years ago now. Did you know it was a great-grandfather of mine who brought the Order of the Assumption to Guatemala?"

"Yes, my daughter, yes. The Reverend Mother told us so."

"He was very rich and wanted his daughters to learn French and follow refined and cultured role models."

"Your mother's behavior must cause your grandmother considerable suffering," the nun interrupted her.

"Mommy is also a good person."

"All right, all right, now tell me the story about the spider."

"No, the centipede one is better."

"As you wish."

Here we go, you fearful old hag.

"Once upon a time there was a centipede," she began reciting with slow deliberation, "who lived in an old shoe, and in the same room there was also a wide, wide bed with a headboard and a mosquito net and a little girl slept there — she looked a lot like me — and the centipede was in love with her. At night when no other sound could be heard — except perhaps the creak of a piece of furniture or a solitary running gutter — it got in through one of the little holes in the mosquito net and drew closer, dragging its hundred legs across the white sheets, until it reached the girl's outstretched arm. Mark was the centipede and I was the little girl," she added, gazing at the nun with a mischievous glint in her eyes, "and the two of us acted out the story."

"I beg your pardon?" Sister Mary Ann reacted with a clatter of needles.

"That's right," said Karen, feeling the familiar tickle that always began in her stomach and carried on down to the tips of her toes. "And as it was dark," she continued, "and the centipede couldn't see me, it slowly climbed all the way up my arm."

"And how did Mark imitate the centipede?" interrupted the nun.

"With his fingers. He slowly crawled up my arm because my skin is all smooth and he liked the way it smelled, and he took short cuts and paused and set off again until he reached my throat and there he'd pause for a long time, and then go on up to my earlobe."

"And did you like it?"

"Yes," replied Karen, "and he caressed the outside of my ear and all the little ridges inside my ear."

"And this went on every night?"

"No, only when I was good, and sometimes instead of his fingers he used the tip of his tongue."

"Enough!" said the nun, setting down her altar cloth again. "It's time we checked over your homework."

"I knew you wouldn't like the story."

"Tomorrow during the break I want you to come with me and scrub the chapel floor. You can offer it up to Our Lord as a penance."

"And what have I done wrong?" asked Karen, widening her eyes.

"Nothing, daughter, nothing. But Our Lord prefers us sometimes to make sacrifices in His Name."

The door opened a fraction, there was a pause, and then it opened a little more.

"Hello," said Karen, "would you like to see what I'm studying?"

"I've decided to tell you a thing or two, and I want you to pay attention," said Natalia, sitting herself down on the bed. She was wearing a red-and-white gingham shirt and navy-blue jeans. She wore her hair up and hardly any make-up.

"How pretty you look. Have you lost weight?"

"Stop being silly, and listen to me. I've come to talk to you about Mark and me, because I think you've got the wrong impression of both of us."

"Oh, yes," said Karen, laying her pencil down on her exercise book, "I'm all ears. Are you going to tell me the fairy tales he's told you?"

"It's not easy," said Natalia, without having heard the question. "You have some very firm and frequently mistaken ideas about the two of us, but I think that in time you'll understand, once you know what love is about."

"If you call what goes on between Mark and you love, believe me, I'd rather be alone. Or do you think you can justify what you've done by softening me up with a word like love?"

"I knew this was going to be difficult, and perhaps the time still isn't right. Did I ever tell you how we first met?"

"I couldn't care less. No doubt Mark was in his smoking jacket and impressed you with his elegant manners and his *savoir faire*."

"See how wrong you are? It wasn't in the least like that. Do you mind if I tell you?"

"Go on then," said Karen, "but not for too long. I've got a lesson at four."

"I was busy vacuuming the carpet," Natalia recalled with a smile, "and I had a towel wrapped around my head because I'd just washed my hair. Suddenly the doorbell rang. It was here in Los Angeles, in the little house with yellow windows. Do you remember it? You'd only just started going to school."

"That place where I broke my tooth on the swing?"

"That's right. I switched off the vacuum cleaner and went to open the door, grumbling. And who do you think was there? — she broke into laughter — "I came face to face with an agitated hen that was flapping its wings and squawking. A face emerged from behind the hen and addressed me with, 'Good day, lady, I would like to introduce you to the hen that laid the eggs that you will have for your breakfast tomorrow morning.' It was Mark. I had to laugh and of course I bought a dozen eggs and he asked for a glass of water and I invited him in with the house in utter chaos. He collapsed into an armchair and asked my permission to take his shoes off because they were pinching him and began to tell me his life story, and how he'd bought 40 dozen eggs and then the hen to use as bait for the customers and that now he had only 15 dozen left. And if when he'd sold them I wanted the hen he'd be willing to give her to me provided he was invited along to the barbecue," she paused for a moment to draw breath. "From the first instant he so charmed me that although I didn't know him, I accepted his proposition."

"And by the next occasion you also accepted his proposition to go to bed, didn't you?"

"Don't be cross," said Natalia. "If I'm telling you all this, it's because I ask myself what would have become of us all if Mark hadn't decided to knock on our door and offer to sell us some eggs."

"We would have been much, much better off," answered Karen, crossing and uncrossing her legs.

"You can't deny that his charm is irresistible," replied Natalia, "you too were under his spell. He sees everything so precisely, so clearly. He always homes in on the important detail. I don't know . . . to me, that ability matters a lot."

"I had a bit much of it myself, and assure you I don't miss it at all."

"Was it a coincidence?" mused Natalia. "How blind I was. No, not blind, selfish. I wanted both things: Mark and you. Above all, Mark."

"Why can't you shut up for once?"

"I pretended not to notice," continued Natalia, ignoring her. "There's always a justification for everything: it's right that you should get used to the idea of poverty, that schools are a waste of time, that Missouri was the only friend you needed. Only Bobby caused me to doubt my superman."

"Why Bobby?" Karen's interest was aroused.

"Nothing," Natalia suddenly came back to earth. "Mark's fine now, working for an insurance company, and in any case I was right to send you here."

"And you still love him when he beats you, when he drags you around by the hair and calls you a whore?"

"Yes, I love him even then. I know that he's hurt you, and hurt me too, but none of that matters. He has an extraordinary refinement, an innate wisdom, and is far more philosophical than any self-styled philosopher."

"You are madder than ever."

"Take it whatever way you want. He's my man and I could never leave him."

"You're completely selfish," said Karen, pacing around the room, "and for you Mark is the only person who counts."

"Your grandmother's right, I did the best thing possible in sending you here."

"You sent me here because you were jealous," Karen stammered as she approached her mother. "You need constant absolution, everyone telling you how right you were to send me here, wanting me to tell you that too, but I won't — do you hear me? — you'll never get me to tell you that."

All at once she noticed she was alone, her head propped against a cold wall. She sobbed against it, chewing on her knuckle as she did so.

"Have you never felt a calling for the religious life?" inquired Sister Mary Ann as the two of them, on their knees, scrubbed the chapel floor.

"No. Why do you ask?"

"No reason, I just wondered."

Karen remained silent.

"Do you still miss Key West?"

"My knees are hurting an awful lot. Couldn't we leave the rest for tomorrow?"

"I've already explained to you that this is a penance," the nun reproved her acerbically. "The Lord will be pleased with you."

"Even though I haven't done anything wrong?"

"The devil never sleeps, and is ever ready to poison us with wicked thoughts when we are idle. But you haven't answered my question. Do you miss Key West?"

"Yes, and above all Missouri."

"And Mark?"

"Him too, he was very amusing."

"There's confession tomorrow, and I think you ought to attend."

"I haven't anything to confess. I went to confession only last week." Karen stretched, her hands on her hips.

"And are you sure you made a full confession to the priest?"

"Yes, of course."

"The centipede story as well?"

"No, but that's not a sin."

"That's true," admitted the nun, blushing, "it wasn't your fault. Tell me one thing, though, when you posed nude for Mark . . ."

"I didn't pose nude, I always wore my underpants."

"All right. When you posed for Mark, did he never try to touch you?"

"Yes, in order to shift my position."

"Where did he touch you?"

"I can't remember any more," replied the girl, going back to scrubbing the floor, "he would tilt my head or my shoulders and rearrange my hair."

"Did your mother know of this?"

"Yes. She told me that photographs were works of art, and that they'd appear in some magazine or other for which Mark would get paid lots of money. I've got some at home, if you'd like me to show you them."

"Yes, I'd like that, but don't let Susan or your other dormitory companions see them, nor even your other teachers."

"Why not? There's nothing wrong with them."

"What does your father make of it?"

"He doesn't like them. He says that Mark and Mommy were corrupting me."

"He's right," pronounced the nun, her eyes fixed firmly on the floor.

"My grandmother likes them. She had one mounted and hung in the living room."

"What did you feel when Mark touched you?" the nun interrupted her.

"Nothing."

"Men are animals. For that reason it would bring me so much pleasure if Our Lord would touch you with His grace."

"Have you ever been touched by a man?"

"Why ask me such questions?"

"You asked me first."

"That's another matter. Well, yes, since you want to know, I underwent the same horrible experience. It was a few months after my father died. My mother and the seven of us children were obliged to go and live in the house of an uncle who was a drunk."

"You see how my mother was right?"

"What about?"

"About the Irish being drunks."

40

"What nonsense," Sister Mary Ann was indignant. "He was the only black sheep in the family."

"All right, go on," said Karen.

"That's got you interested?"

"Yes, very," replied the girl, straightening her back and shaking out her hair.

"Are you tired?"

"A bit, but I want to know what happened."

"Scrub this tile a little harder," the nun pointed to her right, "it's still very dingy."

Karen hobbled on her knees over to the offending tile and began shining it with a dry cloth.

"What time is your first lesson?"

"At four o'clock. After break I've got a study period."

"And do you have a lot of studying to do?"

"No, why?"

"Because I've got a surprise for you," Sister Mary Ann smiled as she picked up the bucket and cloths from the floor. "Come on, follow me."

The two crossed themselves with holy water before leaving the chapel, and handed their utensils to one of the maids who was sweeping the corridor.

What kind of surprise can this be? Karen wondered.

Sister Mary Ann walked ahead of her with hurried steps and seemed to be nervous. They reached the end of the corridor and the nun turned to look in all directions before opening the door with its brown grille.

Could this be possible?

"Come on, quickly," said Sister Mary Ann.

Karen obeyed, and the nun shut the door behind her.

"I thought this was against the rules."

"Shhh," the nun warned, "you need to have a good reason."

"What a beautiful garden."

"Come along, and talk quietly." The nun opened the door to her cell. "Hopefully, no one will notice us."

The cell was narrow and long, its walls were whitewashed and the tiles reddish. There was an iron-framed bed and on it a white cover. Over the bed there hung a wooden crucifix. There was also a narrow closet, a desk and a lone chair.

"Are they all alike?" asked the girl.

"Yes," replied Sister Mary Ann.

"Where would you prefer to sit, on the bed or on the chair?"

"I'm fine here," said Karen, sitting down on the bed.

"We're better off here than in the classroom, don't you think? No one can interrupt us here."

"Are you going to tell me more about your uncle?" Karen asked eagerly.

"If you're interested, yes."

"What's that?" Karen asked, pointing at the desk.

"The coif we wear in bed at night."

"Let me see." She stretched out and wrapped the coif around her head. "Do you have a mirror?"

"How could you imagine such a thing!" The nun was outraged. "When we consecrate our lives to God we renounce worldly vanity, although there may be some" — she laughed with familiar shrillness — "like your beloved Sister Felisa and perhaps Sister Magdalena, who still enjoy admiring themselves. I wouldn't be surprised if either of *them* kept a mirror hidden somewhere."

"They're very pretty," said Karen. "You won't be angry if I ask you something?"

"It depends what."

"I'd like to see your nightshirt."

"What a funny idea, though I don't suppose there's any harm in it," replied the nun, getting up and going over to the closet.

The narrow door creaked open and Karen waited with bated breath. The closet was virtually empty, apart from a habit hung on a peg and a small pile of neatly folded clothes on the shelf.

"Here you are." Sister Mary Ann unfolded her nightshirt. It was made of cloth as thick as a blanket. The color was indefinable, neither white nor beige nor grey. It had a high starched collar and cuffed sleeves.

"And this," added the nun, removing another garment from the closet, "is the shirt in which we take our baths. That way there's no need to appear naked before Our Lord. What else would you like to know?"

"I can't think of anything more for the moment."

She wanted to know what their underclothes were like, but didn't dare ask.

Sister Mary Ann folded up the clothes again and returned them to their closet.

"Don't any of the cells have windows?"

"We have skylights," the nun indicated the ceiling, "but windows would all overlook the garden and distract us from our meditations. "

How warped, thought Karen, adding aloud: "Shall we go on with the story about your uncle?"

"You *are* persistent," the nun smiled as she sat down again. "But all right. Where was I?"

"About how you went to live in your drunken uncle's house."

"Oh yes, now I remember. But it hurts me to think about those things."

"Me too, remembering what Mark did."

"One day I was out in the garden," Sister Mary Ann began, "and my uncle appeared, drunker than ever, and asked me if I was alone. I said yes, that my mother had gone out shopping."

"How old were you?"

"Thirteen or fourteen. At that time I had hair as long as yours and he began to stroke it, asking me why I wasn't at school and tickling me behind my ears."

"What did you feel?"

"A terrible fear."

"And yet at the same time you wanted him to continue, didn't you?"

"No, my child, no. My uncle was panting and snorting and saliva was dribbling from the corners of his mouth. A real wild animal."

"Didn't you tell him to stop?"

"I was paralyzed with terror."

"And then?"

"Such curiosity! I can hardly remember, I've tried to erase the incident from my memory, the only part I still see in my nightmares is his hideous hairy hand inside my blouse. So, anyway, I started screaming and the old degenerate sat down on a bench and attempted to pull me on to his lap. I screamed louder and louder and he covered my mouth with his hand, hurting me, but at that moment my mother arrived."

"What did she do?"

"She told Uncle he was a filthy pig and sent me to my room. The next day I was sent to board at a convent school."

"And she and the rest of your family went on living at your uncle's?"

"Yes. We were very poor, and there was no other option, but they came to visit me every weekend."

"Did you never go out?"

"Very little. Mommy didn't want me to see my uncle again. Then after two years of studying at the convent I felt the call of Our Lord."

Karen felt an uncomfortable flutter in her stomach.

"What's up? You look pale."

"Nothing. I'm a bit tired."

"Let me see if you've got a temperature," said the nun, approaching Karen's side. She placed a hand on her forehead, then on her neck and buried her transparent fingers in Karen's collarbone. "Did you know one can take a pulse by pressing the vein?" The nun was looking at her pocket watch. "No, you don't seem to have a temperature, but it's time for you to go now anyway. I'll come with you."

"Can I come back another time?"

"It's difficult, remember that it's against the rules," replied the nun, poking her head around the door to check the coast was clear. "Hurry up now, nobody's about in the corridor."

"You managed very well today," Mark informed Karen as she was getting ready for bed. "You achieved the impossible, you transformed the old dragon into a sacrificial lamb."

"What makes you say that?"

"Haven't you noticed how tenderly she treats you, taking you to her cell, giving you grades you haven't really earned, and telling you what a good girl you are, when only three months ago she regarded you as untamed and even possibly retarded? Be careful, or you'll end up a nun too."

"Why not? Maybe Our Lord will touch me with His grace."

"Don't be ridiculous," Mark was laughing. "Do you want to corrupt all the priests? Being a nun must be the most boring thing in the world, and you weren't born for that."

"So what *was* I born for?"

"How would I know? Perhaps to be a beautiful young woman, even more beautiful than your mother, to travel and have lots of friends and one day to marry someone as smart as me, then every night to tell him stories like Scheherazade. He'll listen entranced, one night playing Lancelot to your Guinevere, and the next Merlin the enchanter to your Morgana . . . do you remember how you used to love being Morgana when I'd open the window to chart the stars and you would threaten me with your spells? Still, I suspect the story you liked best was about the spider, am I right?"

"No, you're wrong."

"Would you like me to tell you it again?"

"Yes," Karen said in a whisper so soft as to be almost inaudible, as she covered her face with the sheets.

"Fine, Miss Muffet," said Mark, coming a little closer, and Karen: "Did you give Bolita to Miss Muffet?" And Mark: "Once upon a time there was a spider —" and Karen: "No, we'd better not —" and Mark: "who lived in a very old house —" and Karen: "I've already told you to stop, I'm getting frightened —" and Mark, without paying any attention: "and his legs were very hairy —" and Karen again felt Mark's hand sliding beneath the sheets and touching her ankle, then slowly climbing her leg like the spider, slowly but with little jumps, slowly but always climbing, and Karen was frightened and wanted to burst out laughing and wanted him both to stop and to go on, and Mark: "You really miss me, don't you?"

"No," she said, opening her eyes and feeling her tongue all swollen, "and I've told you before I don't like your stories."

"Bobby, how did Bobby die?" whispered Karen to nobody from the depths of her chair. "Instead of going to the cinema that afternoon I should have stayed at home."

She took a deep breath, held it and squeezed her eyelids together. A ritual that sometimes worked.

It was three in the afternoon and Mark appeared in the bedroom.

"Natalia, I want you to come drinking with me."

Bobby got up off the floor, yawned, slowly stretched himself and went to greet Mark waving his tail around like a corkscrew.

"What do you think," asked Mark, "of our selling off what little we possess and going to Coconut Island to dig for buried treasure?"

Natalia smiled as she smoothed the covers over the bed.

"See? All you do is smile. You don't even consider doing it, do you? I can't even communicate with you, and as for you, you only respond to me when I hurt you," he added, squeezing her wrist, "that's the only time I feel you're actually real. Come to the living room. I've told you, we're going to get drunk together."

He poured out two glasses with a steady hand, sank into the yellow chair and Bobby leapt up beside him.

"Cheers," he said, raising his glass.

"Cheers," she murmured from the sofa.

"What's up?" he asked, "would you prefer rum?"

"No, it's all the same to me."

"I want to talk to you about my new film," he caressed the rim of his glass, "but first I'll expound my theory of humanity to you."

46

Natalia pulled her legs up on to the sofa, folding them under her skirt.

"Wake up, baby, gin gets the blood coursing and I want you to hear what I have to say."

She swallowed a sip. To Karen it seemed as though she did so unwillingly.

"This is the way I like you," Mark was watching her with a smile somewhere between tenderness and mockery, "you see, all week I've been thinking about how humanity has sunk into a pit for the simple reason that most people — starting from childhood — are so gullible. If I told Karen, for example, that the moon is made of green cheese, she wouldn't doubt it for a moment and it'd take years and years for her to be convinced that really . . ."

"Maybe it is," Natalia interrupted, "maybe it's an enormous round of Roquefort." "

"Drop the idiocies, I'm being serious. It takes years to persuade someone that Father Christmas doesn't exist, that there are no fairy godmothers and the moon is only a round stone rotating in space. Most people allow themselves to be captivated by lies like these."

"So much the better."

"Don't interrupt," said Mark, serving himself another glass while Natalia secretly poured some of hers into the pot of hydrangeas beside her.

"Not many people manage to break free of such lies," Mark continued, "and to see the world as it actually is. Only these are privileged to enjoy life and indulge in its better moments."

"There might be more than one version of reality. As well as that we experience, there is another that we dream, and another we invent."

"I've already told you to stop interrupting."

"I thought you wanted a conversation."

Bobby lifted his head as, with his free hand, Mark tickled him behind the ears.

"What was I saying? You cut off the flow of my inspiration."

"Something about people breaking free of lies."

"Right." He took another gulp. "Speaking in general terms, humanity can be divided into two groups: the somnambulant simpletons who want to be told bedtime stories to sleep more soundly, and the intelligent ones capable of inventing the stories and picking the pockets of the unsuspecting ones. What do you think?" He got up from his chair and began pacing the room.

She didn't reply.

"Come on, what do you think?"

"You won't be angry if I tell you?"

"No, why should I be angry?"

"Because even the intelligent ones fall flat from time to time."

Mark wandered over to the window with his glass and Natalia hurriedly emptied the contents of hers into the plant pot.

"You're right," said Mark, returning to his armchair.

"Another Martini?"

"No, not yet."

He poured himself another glass from the jug, settled into the armchair and leaned his head back thoughtfully.

"The difference is that they return to the fray with greater energy," he said after a pause, "any fall impels them to rise again higher. In contrast the rest remain inert or continue to wallow in their abyss of quicksand. Come on, drink with me," he added, filling her glass.

"Why don't you resume work on your documentary?" she asked, sipping her drink.

"Because I'm more interested in my private project." He shot her an ironic look and scratched Bobby's neck, "Would you like us to work on it?"

"No, I'm not in the mood."

"Oh come on," he cajoled, going to sit beside her on the sofa, "the camera is all set up."

"Karen will be back shortly."

Mark nuzzled her neck and she brusquely moved her head away.

"You never feel in the mood nowadays," he was becoming irritated, "what you need is a sound thrashing."

"How's the film going with Karen?"

"You'll see it when it's done — assuming, of course, that Karen gives her permission."

Natalia shifted uncomfortably on the sofa.

"You're jealous, aren't you?"

"Don't be absurd," she said, getting up.

"Where are you going?"

"To the bathroom. I'll be back."

Mark also got up and returned to the open window.

After a few minutes he called out: "Why are you taking so long?"

"Be right there."

Rays of light flooded into the room, lighting up the furniture, the Cuevas engraving, the nape of Mark's neck, a spider's web dangling from the ceiling, and the fine dust coating the surface of a blue vase.

"Why are you standing over there?" he asked, turning his head.

"No reason," she said, returning to the sofa once more. "I was admiring the nape of your neck."

"It's impossible to discuss anything with women, Bobby," complained Mark, returning to his armchair.

"Go on, then," she said wearily.

"Fill up your glass, I've already warned you that we're going to get drunk together."

She obeyed and he, glass in hand, walked over to the window again.

She emptied half the glassful into the plant pot.

"Why do you deceive me?" he asked with his back still turned. "Do you think I'm not wise to your tricks?"

He approached her slowly, rubbing his teeth with his index finger. He placed the glass on the table and slapped her cheek with the flat of his hand.

She attempted to get up from the sofa, but he struck her again and she lost her balance and fell to the floor. Bobby, who had begun leaping up at them, started barking, eyeing Mark.

"Get out, you miserable mutt," shouted Mark.

Natalia made another attempt to rise and Mark again toppled her with a kick.

"Coward," she said as she finally struggled to her feet. Mark began hitting her again and Bobby got in between them.

"Fucking dog!" Mark swore and ran to the kitchen for a broom.

She ran to the bathroom, locking the door and securing the window.

"Get out, you blasted dog!" Mark started whacking Bobby with the broom. Bobby retreated to the patio, whimpering. Mark kept on hitting him, howling in a thick voice: "Fucking dog, fucking treacherous dog!"

Natalia half opened the window. "Stop it Mark," she pleaded, "you'll end up killing him."

Mark carried on with the vicious attack. Suddenly Bobby bared his fangs and snarled at Mark.

"All right," Mark dropped the broom, "now you've asked for it."

He shut the kitchen door and went into the bedroom.

"Where the devil have you put my revolver?" he called from inside.

She didn't answer.

"Where in hell have you put it?" he bawled, turning over the closet.

"Run away, Bobby," she begged, gazing in terror at the dog cowering in a corner.

"You don't even have enough imagination to hide a revolver," taunted Mark, crossing the patio. He noisily slammed the kitchen door and two rapid shots rang out, followed by a piercing howl from Bobby and another shot. Natalia opened the door and ran half-crazed towards the dog.

"Don't go near him," said Mark, pointing the gun at her, "or I'll shoot you too."

"Do what you like, superman," she answered clenching her teeth and kneeling beside Bobby, who still managed to gaze back at her through the blue and gelatinous haze that was filming over his pupils.

"Do you know something, Daddy?" asked Karen as they were driving along the freeway. "I don't want to go back to school."

"The things you say," said her father, turning to look at her, "you really pick your moment."

Karen remained silent as interminable rows of houses, all indistinguishable, rushed past her eyes. Not a single patch of open ground; the surroundings were hideous.

"What are you thinking?"

"How ugly this landscape is."

"What's going on, Karen?"

"Nothing. I just don't like school."

"But it's barely a week since you told me you were happy there."

"I told you that to please you."

"And what would you do if I took you out of school?"

"Find another one not run by nuns."

"You're a difficult girl," her father sighed, "the nuns are doing their utmost to set you straight and I admit I'm pretty pleased with the results. Last month your grades were very good."

"I promised you I'd study."

"What don't you like about it? It's among the most expensive schools in California and they're very selective about whom they admit."

"I know. They only take rich girls."

"And what do you have against rich girls? Friendships made at your age are very important for the rest of your life."

"They spend their time discussing clothes and boyfriends and stuff that doesn't interest me."

"You'll become interested," he smiled, "I want you to meet some boys of your own age this summer. What else don't you like?"

"I don't like any of it. The food is revolting. Every morning it's cereal and cold eggs and at lunchtime rice like glue and for supper meat that's impossible to chew. Even Susan says it's horsemeat, and for her to complain there must be something wrong."

"You like Susan, don't you?"

"She's a good friend and always does her best to help me out," said Karen, "but she spends all her time studying and she's really square."

"It wouldn't be a bad idea if you squared up a bit, don't you think?"

It's impossible to talk to him, thought Karen. What was it Mark used to say? "A jerk who devoted his life to selling real estate isn't so much a square as a soggy doughnut with a vast hole in the middle." What must he dream of?

"And what can you tell me about Sister Mary Ann?"

"Frustrated like the rest of them."

"The poor nun must have something going for her."

"Yes, her eyes," Karen remarked enthusiastically," she has the weirdest eyes, and when she looks at you you can see golden flecks flashing from them."

"Don't be unfair. The Reverend Mother says Sister Mary Ann actually lies awake at night thinking up ways of helping you, and that she has rarely encountered such self-abnegation."

"She tries to pin me to her side all day long in order to monitor me. She's a gossip who envies all the others."

"Come on, don't exaggerate. Just finish the year like you promised me, and we'll think again during the holidays."

Karen huddled into her seat and said nothing.

"How does that sound?"

"As you wish. Are you going to send me to a summer camp, or back to Grandmother in Guatemala?"

"That depends on all sorts of things, but if you continue working as hard as you are, you can choose for yourself."

"I'd like to go to Guatemala."

"In Yosemite there's the loveliest campsite where you can swim and ride and do a thousand other things."

I've lost again, thought Karen, closing her eyes. Every time common sense wins out, solidity, the hole in the doughnut.

"What does this picture mean?" inquired Sister Mary Ann, her voice as sharp as before.

Of all the lessons, Karen's favorite was art.

"I'm not sure," she replied almost in a whisper, "don't you like it?"

"You've drawn it well," replied the nun, scrutinizing it with a frown, "but what an image: a knife buried in someone's back!"

Karen remained silent and the nun put the drawing down on the desk.

"Why did you do it? Examine it carefully. Perhaps you harbor the desire to stab somebody? It's a woman's back."

"It was just a memory."

"Don't you want to tell me?"

"Okay, if you're interested. It was in the house with the little blue doors in Key West. I'd spent the day on the beach with Missouri."

"With whom?"

"With my black friend."

"Oh him," the nun sounded impatient.

"Bolita, the dog who now belongs to Miss Muffet, was with us, amusing herself digging vast holes in the sand. At around four o'clock we went to tea at Nicolasa's house, as Mommy and Mark had gone out on the motorbike and there was nothing to eat. Nicolasa had told me to come to her house any time I felt hungry and sometimes she gave me eggs from her favorite hen, and chicken, and bread she had baked herself."

"Am I right in thinking that Nicolasa is Missouri's mother?" asked the nun, compressing her lips into a narrow white line.

"Yes, and she had eleven children and said that one more was no trouble, and Missouri dropped me home at nine o'clock and Mark and Mommy still hadn't arrived. I was afraid and thought that something must have happened to them. Mark raced a lot on his motorbike, he said it was a wonderful sensation, almost like flying."

"And your mother allowed you out on the motorbike with him, didn't she?"

"Yes, although at first she was worried, but she ended up getting used to the idea and I enjoyed it too."

"And that night Missouri stayed with you?"

"No, he only brought me as far as the house, and I was scared and couldn't get to sleep, although in the end I went to sleep with Bolita at my feet and didn't hear them get home. I had a very odd dream" — Karen's voice sounded foggy — "I dreamed that Missouri and I were walking through a wood and suddenly the trees thinned out and it became a labyrinth and Missouri was no longer Missouri; he was Mark and he kept laughing and I was afraid. Then Mark was no longer Mark; he turned into a huge black dog that stood up on its hind legs in front of me and I suddenly woke up and heard a noise coming from Mommy's room. The light was on and — no, I don't think I should go on" — her normal voice had returned — "you'll be annoyed with me."

"Don't be silly, why would I be annoyed?"

"I got up and opened the door quietly and there was Mommy sitting very upright in bed, and Mark with a knife in his hand, a knife with an ivory handle given to him by his father. He was Lying across the bed laughing and running the blade of the knife up and down Mommy's spine."

"Oh no!" exclaimed the nun. "And was your mother dressed or naked?"

"Naked, and so was Mark. Neither of them knew I was there."

"Why didn't you leave? One should never have to witness such things."

"Because I couldn't figure out if Mark was playing with Mommy or if he was thinking of killing her. Mommy's back was so rigid it didn't give anything away, and Mark kept laughing so that they didn't hear when I opened the door. In the end I called out to Mommy and she calmly turned to look at me and told me to go back to bed, that it was only a game, and Mark kept right on laughing without getting annoyed with me. And I asked if I could stay, but Mommy said no, that I should go to my room. She never liked me to get mixed up in their games. Sometimes she would laugh a lot, but this time she was serious and it seemed to me she was afraid."

"And next day did neither of them apologize to you?"

"No, Mark only said that maybe one day he'd teach me the game, but he never did."

"And you were unaffected by seeing them naked?"

"I often saw them like that. Mark always said there was no reason to be ashamed of our bodies."

"Oh no," the nun repeated, "have you told your father about this?"

"No, he'd only get cross with Mommy."

"And did you and Missouri ever get undressed together?"

"Just once, when we were both eleven, and I'd just arrived at Key West."

"Did he do anything to you?" Sister Mary Ann's eyes were agitated. "Didn't he try to touch you?"

"No, we simply laughed a lot and after a while I put my bikini back on."

"Bikini!" The nun was outraged. "How *can* the youth of today parade around bare-skinned, inciting the devil?"

"The Bible says that Adam and Eve walked about naked," Karen protested.

Sister Mary Ann gave a deep sigh and crossed her hands in her lap.

"The Lord loves you deeply," she said. "He it was who desired you to escape from the wicked surroundings in which you found .yourself."

"It wasn't wicked."

"Listen to me, my child," said the nun without paying attention, "each time such memories come to mind, try to suppress them, and instead of letting your imagination express itself in a drawing, recite a decade of the rosary or come and talk to me. Remember I'm your spiritual adviser and that everything concerning you concerns me. Now how about reading a few pages of the life of our little St. Therese together?"

Karen was already in bed, thinking how fed up she was with the life of the blessed saint, when Mark's laugh suddenly erupted.

"What are you doing here?" she said, snuggling down into bed.

"I've only come for a moment, to offer my congratulations."

Karen kept quiet.

"You were perfect with the nun. You did exactly what's necessary to keep her attached to your apron strings, by talking to her in all innocence of matters you know are guaranteed to scandalize her."

"You're perverse."

"Would you like to know something, a few last words of advice? Pretend that the little way of that saint fascinates you and that you'd do anything to be like her. Then, when you've really softened her up, tell her about the boat. They'll have no choice but to expel you, you'll be far too dangerous to have alongside the other girls."

"You're bad. Does Mommy know all about the boat?"

"Of course," Mark burst out laughing, "she was watching it all from the beach."

"And she still goes on loving you?"

"I'm the only thing she cares about."

"I don't believe you, she cares about me too or else she wouldn't keep writing all those letters to me."

"Pangs of conscience." Mark was laughing at her again.

"You're bad and I don't want to see you again. You killed Bobby, didn't you?"

"How could you imagine such a thing? Why on earth would I kill him? I've already told you he got stolen, he was a very beautiful dog."

"You're lying," said Karen, sitting bolt upright. "When I got home that night Mommy's eyes were all red from crying so much and she didn't want to talk to you and called you a murderer."

"Your mother is subject to occasional attacks of hysteria."

"I can't understand what she sees in you."

"You'll understand all right when you're older," he said, drawing closer. "Do you know something? Your mother sent you away because she was jealous."

"You're lying, you're lying!" Karen screamed as she buried her head in the pillow, "you make me sick and you're drunk" — she shot him a glance through half-closed eyes — "why don't you get out and never come back?"

"Karen, Karen," said Susan, "what's going on?"

Karen turned to face the wall and feigned sleep.

Next day she said she was feeling ill and didn't go down to the dining room at breakfast time. She began furiously brushing her hair in front of the mirror above the washbasin. Then she took a comb, made a center parting and pulled locks of hair down over her eyes.

Great, she said to herself, now I need to paint rings around my eyes and add some crows' feet. She took a piece of charcoal and began drawing. Brilliant, now I only need the glasses and books to complete the image.

She helped herself to Susan's glasses, put three books under each arm and regarded herself triumphantly in the mirror.

"Karen," said Natalia, "what are you doing?"

"Surprised?" Karen asked in a deeper, more mature voice.

"Yes, I was sure you'd go on being as flirtatious as ever."

"I tried until I was twenty and it never worked out," she replied, looking coldly at her mother.

"Am I to blame for that too?"

"Naturally," said Karen, dropping the books on to the bed. "You knew that Mark used to come into my room at night and you never concerned yourself with what we might be getting up to."

"I know he told you stories."

"Don't play the idiot." Karen was irritated. "Didn't he tell you that to make it all more entertaining he would act them out on my body?"

"What's wrong with that?"

"It's clear you just don't want to understand. Any more than you wanted to take an interest in the film we were making together."

"Neither of you ever let me. You made out it was top secret and that nobody else could come in on it."

"Did you never watch a single reel?"

"Yes, just recently Mark showed me some."

"And what did you make of it?" Karen asked, her voice hoarse.

"That you were delicious. You looked like Perugino's Magdalen."

"'Nothing more erotic than a pre-pubescent,' Mark would say as he fiddled with my hair and accidentally brushed my breasts with his arm."

"Why didn't you ever tell me?"

"Because I liked it. The sensation of mixed terror and curiosity attracted me and I didn't want you to prohibit it. But now I'm frigid, lying like a wooden log next to whoever I'm with, I feel disgusted and afraid."

"That's the way I was with your father. No woman is frigid with a man who knows how to arouse her."

"You learned that stock sentence from Mark, didn't you?"

Natalia nodded.

"Grandmother did you far less harm telling you that sex was dirty than you did to me by exposing me to Mark's lechery."

"I never dreamt . . ."

"You're lying" — Karen was shouting passionately — "you're lying because it suits you to lie, it lets you off any sense of guilt. If you didn't know what was happening, why did you send me to Daddy in California?"

"Because —" Natalia was hesitating as she found somewhere to sit down, "because I sensed that a certain antagonism was developing between Mark and you; also he was drinking and opposed your going to school and so I thought you'd be better off here."

"Don't be a hypocrite, Mommy. You knew perfectly well what happened on the boat and you never made a point of talking to me but decided that it was easiest for you to send me off and get me and my problems out of the way. You did it far less for my own good than out of jealousy."

"Don't be ridiculous." Natalia was blinking rapidly.

"You know I'm telling the truth and there's no way your crocodile tears are going to impress me now. At best Mark found my innocence and curiosity provocative, but he ended up really terrifying me. The scene on the boat is one I remember every time a man wants to caress me. I've seen a psychiatrist and it's been no help at all. It's your fault I'm so wretched and anyone who loves me is made wretched too."

Natalia said nothing.

"And there's another happy memory that comes to mind clearly on these occasions. Do you remember the brothels where you used to take me in search of Mark every time he disappeared? You and I walking the slums of Guatemala city after Grandfather threw you out of the house, going into one bar after another, all smelling of vomit and cheap perfume with the women lined up on benches with their legs spread and skirts hoisted up to their waists, looking at us with hatred and catcalling at us. The men's eyes roving over your body as I looked on in fright, their stares, all sorts of stares: reproving, covetous, pitying, amused or scornful, and all you did was take me by the hand and continue searching. It wasn't only their stares but also their whispers and obscene remarks, and me my eyes stretched open with sleepiness — telling you: 'I'm tired' and you taking no notice: 'I think it must be this one,' and you'd go in there with your heart turning cartwheels, and it'd be another, always another, and I'd be whimpering: 'I can't go on, Mommy,' but you'd keep going, ceaselessly repeating: 'What could have happened to him?'"

"Mark is a helpless child," whispered Natalia.

"Don't come to me now with your pat phrases."

"You loathe me, don't you?"

Karen remained silent.

"Unbelievable! You're nearly naked," Sister Mary Ann was working up to a fine pitch of indignation as she intently studied the photos, "who made you up? Your face looks like a mask."

"Mark."

"I guessed as much. It shows what kind of a human being he is, wanting to turn you into an object of his lasciviousness. Praise be to God for having saved you from such a beast. Haven't you noticed how much prettier you are like this, your own face clean and natural, without affectation?" The nun was looking at her tenderly. "Why do you think your mother found it necessary to send you away so suddenly?"

Karen offered no reply beyond a shrug of her shoulders.

"Why don't we have a read of St. Therese?" she asked. "I love reading about her and would like to take her as my model."

"Very well," said Sister Mary Ann, putting the photos away in her pocket, "but first I have something to show you. Do you really want to take St. Therese as your model?" she added, rummaging in the bag where she kept her needlework.

"Yes, but I don't think I'll manage it."

"Anything can be achieved with patience," replied Sister Mary Ann, taking out a metal object with leather straps. "Do you know what this is?"

"Let's see," the girl stretched out her hand.

"My mother gave it to me the day I took my vows."

It was a rectangular wire mesh with the jagged edges turned inwards and two leather straps to hold it in place. Karen examined it carefully.

"What's it for?" she finally asked.

"It's called an instrument of mortification," said the nun, her face suddenly radiant, "and it serves to prove our love for Our Lord."

Karen contemplated the object blankly.

"Look," Sister Mary Ann explained, removing it from her grasp, "you attach it like this," and she put it on around her waist, tying the leather straps at the back. "Of course you should only wear it against your bare flesh."

"Don't the edges hurt?"

"That's what it's for, my child," Sister Mary Ann turned to look at her with a beatific smile, "but you offer the pain up to Our Lord."

"If it hurts you so much, why do you tell me all this looking so joyful?"

"Whatever sacrifice we make to Our Lord bestows an infinite joy upon us. Do you want to try it on?"

Karen put it on over her uniform. "Not like that, it has to be against your flesh."

"No," said Karen, shaking.

"Look here," said the nun, her voice marginally less harsh than usual, rolling up the sleeves of her habit and blouse. "There are instruments of mortification for your arms and your legs as well, and I've got them all. Look at the marks they've left behind."

Karen stared with horror at the bruised blotches etched into the nun's withered and yellowed skin.

"And did St. Therese go in for this too?"

"Of course, my child, these and no doubt many other far more painful mortifications we daren't even imagine, and yet see how her face radiates sublime joy."

"Let me look again."

"Here, take it whenever you want."

Karen examined the thing again with a mixture of horror and fascination, and discovered that the edges bore traces of dried blood. She gave it back to the nun without a word.

"Most chaste Mother of us all," recited the priest, echoed by a chorus of nuns, teachers and pupils.

"Mother most pure, Mother most fearless."

Karen narrowed her eyes and found herself watching the candle flames flowing in all directions, illuminating the priest's face and dancing to the sound of his voice that echoed terrifyingly around the walls.

Wah, wah, she remembered Jet's barking echoing around the garage walls.

"Karen," said her mother, tiptoeing into the room where Karen lay asleep, "get up without making a sound, Mark wants to see you."

"Mmm," she muttered and turned over. "What's going on?"

"Nothing, don't make any noise or you'll wake your grandparents, hurry."

Karen unwillingly got out of her bed, put on her slippers and followed her mother down the west passageway.

"At last," said Mark, jingling the ice in his glass, "I want you to remove your slippers immediately."

"Mark," protested Natalia, "it's raining."

"Shut up, you." Mark shot her an angry look.

"Now go out into the yard," Mark went on, "and bring me Jet."

Karen was rooted to the spot, petrified.

"What are you waiting for?" asked Mark. "I told you to bring me Jet."

"I'll come too," said Natalia.

"Star of the Morning," continued the priest.

Karen squeezed her eyes more firmly shut. From the bottom of each candle extended a green light, and the chapel began to turn into an aquarium and the nuns into praying mantis.

"No," Mark grabbed one of Natalia's arms, and she lost her balance, "you're not going anywhere."

Karen looked at her mother and turned away again, like an automaton.

"Don't go, Karen, don't go," implored Natalia, "Jet will kill you."

"Shut up, will you!" yelled Mark.

"Why don't you go?" shrieked Karen.

"One more word and you'll have to bring me the whip." Mark was staring into her eyes.

"Grandmother, Grandmother!" Karen cried as she fled barefoot down the passageway.

"Damn girl!" growled Mark.

"Tower of ebony," said the priest, and Grandmother arrived, wrapping herself in her dressing-gown.

Karen's forehead was bathed in a cold sweat.

"Pervert!" screamed the grandmother. "You know all too well how that dog hates children."

"Queen of Peace," said the priest.

The rain went on falling on to the yard, on to the garage, on to the chapel roof.

"Come here, Karen," said her grandmother, running over to her, hugging her and taking her to her bedroom. Karen squeezed her eyelids almost completely shut, and thousands of rays and red sparks darted from the flames. Mark was like a vengeful god, demanding that his word should be obeyed by all.

"Mother most wise," recited the priest, and Natalia's bare footsteps could be heard in the distance.

"So long as you're with me, he won't touch a hair of your head," said Grandmother, and Karen leaned against her. They could still hear Natalia's pattering feet and wah, wah, Jet's barking.

"She's as mad as he is," whispered her grandmother, and the priest's voice stopped. The rays and the little sparks went out and the faces of Grandmother, Mark and Natalia went out too. Karen opened her eyes and the priest put his hands together and the nuns, teachers and girls stood up and waited for the priest to go into the sacristy before filing out, their heads covered with white mantillas. The verger put out the candles and the chapel again began to transform itself, this time into a prison-yard where rows of benches were arranged for the sinners awaiting God who at any moment would appear, scales in hand. Some would be sent to heaven and others to hell and nobody could do anything about it, and the yard filled up with smoke and the odor of candle smoke and sanctity.

"Sister Mary Ann, Sister Mary Ann!" Karen was running along after the nun.

Sister Mary Ann paused and turned to look at her.

"What's up? Why the hurry?"

"Can we go to the classroom?" Karen was almost out of breath, "I've got something to tell you."

"It's time for prayers, but very well, if it's important."

"I think so, very important."

"Very well then, go ahead. I'll be with you in a moment."

Waiting made Karen nervous.

"I can't be with you long," said Sister Mary Ann, going over to her chair, "I came simply because it's something specifically to do with you."

"Thank you," said Karen, rising.

"Sit down, sit down," said the nun, "we've no time to waste."

Do you remember," began Karen, "that in our last session you asked me the reason why Mommy sent me here and I didn't want to answer?"

"I remember."

"I think now I know. After examining my conscience I decided not to conceal anything any longer because you always offer advice that's for my own good." Karen opened her eyes wide and felt a shiver of evil. "You won't scold me or make me clean the chapel on my knees?"

"No, my child, no."

"Mark was drunk and invited us to spend the day in the bay. When we arrived, he said it was a perfect day for going out

64

in the boat and that he was going to hire a dinghy. It could only hold two people and Mark insisted on my going with him and helped me in. He asked Mommy if she'd brought the oil and she started turning out her basket to find it. 'Here,' she said, 'here it is, and please go carefully.'

Mark began to take the boat out, and after a while he asked, 'Do you want to row for a bit? Sit down facing me.'

The oars were very heavy, but he placed his hands over mine and that made it easier.

How kind Mark is, I thought, and how much he must love me."

Karen looked again at Sister Mary Ann to observe what effect her words were having.

"'The lagoon is very calm,' said Mark after a pause, 'we can relax and let the boat drift. Do you want a swim?'

'No,' I said, 'I'm frightened and the water's too deep.'

Mark laughed and took a swig from his bottle, then offered me one. I said no thanks and what about poor Mommy, he should take her out later. He didn't answer and after a while said we ought to put some oil on our bodies as the sun was burning.

'You oil me, and I'll oil you.'"

"The degenerate," hissed the nun.

"I picked up the bottle from the bottom of the boat," Karen continued, "poured a little oil in the palm of my hand, and began to rub it into his shoulders, arms and back.

'Do you want me to put some on your legs and stomach too?' I asked.

'Of course, you mustn't leave anywhere out,' he replied.

By the time I'd finished, I'd used up more than half the bottle.

'Now it's my turn,' he said, laying aside the oars, 'lie face downwards.'"

"Oh my God," murmured the nun, and Karen felt an overwhelming urge to burst out laughing.

"I obeyed," she innocuously continued, "and he began rubbing my shoulders and back and tickling my armpits.

'What a beautiful back you have,' he said, 'if your looks hold you'll end up a professional model,' and he kissed the small of my back."

"You didn't object?"

"No, I felt so relaxed and I didn't think there could be any harm in it."

"Very well. Continue."

"'Turn over,' he ordered after a while, 'it's your tummy's turn.'

'You have a sensational belly button,' he told me, moving his finger around like this, 'very deep, just as I like them.'"

"Satan incarnate!" exclaimed the nun.

"I screamed and told him not to, but he kissed me on the mouth and began rubbing one of my breasts."

Sister Mary Ann covered her face with her hands and muttered something inaudible.

"As we were struggling he pulled down my straps and kissed my nipple."

"Enough!" cried the nun.

"I pulled his hair as hard as I could," continued Karen, ignoring her, "and he told me not to be stupid, that this was a much better game than any I'd played so far, one that only grown-ups played."

"Enough, enough!" repeated Sister Mary Ann.

"He put his hand underneath my bikini and I shouted louder and I couldn't think how to escape. And although I'm not a very good swimmer I threw myself into the water and began swimming away with all my strength."

"You poor little angel!"

"Mark yelled something I couldn't hear and began to row in the opposite direction and I couldn't go on any more, I felt my legs caught in the duckweed and began to swallow water. My head was coming up and then going under water again, and in the end Mark brought the boat over and helped me in and called me stupid. He laid me out on my back on the floor and began to give me artificial respiration and I vomited and started crying."

"Have mercy, Lord," sighed the nun.

"And then I vomited again and he wouldn't help me and when we reached shore Mommy was hysterical because she'd seen me almost drown. She wrapped me up in a towel and we went home in a rented car and I locked myself in my room and wouldn't have dinner or see anyone. The next day Mark banged on my window but I paid no attention and went for over a week refusing to see him."

"I don't blame you."

"Afterwards I wouldn't talk to him and he said he was sorry and bought me presents and I didn't open them. Even my mother would scarcely speak to him and called him an animal in front of me."

"Did you discuss this in detail with your mother?" asked the nun.

"No," replied Karen. "Once I tried telling her Mark absolutely terrified me, but she said it was only because he'd been drunk and didn't know what he was doing, and that I should try and forget it."

"How could she?" whispered the nun.

"Then one night she came into my room to tell me I was going away to spend some time with my father. Don't you think it was because of this?"

"At least she finally saw the light, you were in the most terrible danger."

"Daddy doesn't know."

"And Susan?"

"Nor her."

"It'd be better not to tell her."

"Do you think it might give her sinful thoughts?" Karen inquired with feigned innocence.

"Yes, child, yes, there's no reason to discuss these matters. Are you quite certain that you only experienced fear when he started to take advantage of you?"

"I think so."

"Men are wild animals," Sister Mary Ann rose and caressed Karen's hair. "Come with me, we'll say our prayers together in the chapel."

After a disgusting meal of spaghetti and meatballs, Karen felt ill and was taken off to the infirmary.

At about four o'clock Sister Mary Ann arrived to see her. No one else was around. The nurse had diagnosed indigestion and given her an emetic.

Karen was half asleep when she sensed someone sitting at her bedside. She opened her eyes and tried to sit up.

"Rest, my child, rest," said the nun, placing her hand on her forehead, "how do you feel?"

"Better since I vomited."

"Are you strong enough for some good news?" the nun smiled.

Karen nodded.

"You've won the prize of honor, and as it will be announced tomorrow, I wanted to let you know beforehand."

Karen began to tremble. A miracle, she thought, can it really be true? Daddy will be so pleased.

"Aren't you going to say anything?" asked the nun.

"Did I truly earn it?"

"Yes, my daughter, yes. You were first in history, social studies, drawing and mathematics. What do you think of that?"

"Fantastic!" said Karen, and struggled up to embrace the nun.

"Calm down," Sister Mary Ann gently pushed her back, "I've not finished yet. Look," and she took from her pocket a scapular embroidered with the Sacred Heart. "Do you know what it's for?"

"Yes, Susan has one. It's a talisman to ward off evil. It's called a 'deten,' for *detente Sétanas,* Get Thee Behind Me, Satan."

"Precisely," said the nun, holding it out to Karen, "I want you always to wear it. You've earned the prize of honor, but I'll give you this talisman in its place."

"Why?" asked Karen in distress.

"Because I don't want you to become vain."

"But I've always had low grades, all the girls know that, and now . . ."

"Listen," the nun interrupted her. "You and I know you have earned the prize of honor and this talisman is the proof. It's a sacrifice I'm asking you to make to Our Lord."

"It's not fair," said Karen in a voice that trembled, looking absently at the talisman she was holding in her hands. "I worked so hard for my father's sake, I want to give him this pleasure."

"You'll offer it up to Our Lord, and that's even more important."

"I don't want to! I don't want to!" Karen threw herself on to the bed, thrashing her legs.

"Don't carry on like this. I embroidered it myself." The nun was stroking her hair.

"It's not fair, it's not fair!" Karen sobbed and continued kicking.

"Forgive me, my child. I mean it for your own good."

"I'll never study again, from now on I'll always come last and to hell with my father and with you and the Reverend Mother."

"Don't say such things!" The nun was alarmed. "I should have spoken to you earlier but unfortunately I've already returned the certificate."

Karen began pounding the pillow with her fists.

"Come, come," said the nun, taking out her handkerchief. "Let me dry your tears."

"It's not fair, it's not fair," repeated Karen, taking no notice of her.

"You know how dearly I love you." The nun leaned over the girl. "You of all people are closest to my heart. Look what I have for you here." She put her hand in her pocket.

Karen looked again. It was one of her photos.

"I'll take them away this very day, I don't want you to have them."

"No child, no. Don't deprive me of this." The nun replaced her hand on the girl's head. "I sleep with them under my pillow, so l can be close to you always. Would you like me to read you a little of the life of St. Therese?" she added in a shaky voice, her eyes darting feverishly around the room.

"No," said Karen, who had stopped crying. "Her life is as boring as all the rest of your saints."

The talisman suddenly caught her eye and she squeezed it in her fist. It's hers, she thought, squeezing it harder, and it's here within my grasp.

"Or would you rather have a story?" asked the nun, almost in a whisper.

Sister Mary Ann's heart here in my hand.

"Once upon a time there was a very ugly toad who lived at the bottom of the garden," the nun began in an uncertain voice, "the poor little chap was misshapen and terribly ordinary."

In my hand, I've got it right here in my hand. I can destroy it if I wish.

The nun's hand jerked clumsily from Karen's head to her neck.

Karen shuddered.

"But in reality the toad was a beautiful fairy that had been turned into a toad by a cruel and wicked magician who was furious with her for never paying any attention to him. Instead of going to his parties the toad hopped across the garden every day to wait for a girl who always arrived with her books under her arm and stretched out on the lawn to study them."

"And did the girl look like me?"

"Yes, darling, yes," said the nun, and the toad caressed Karen's cheek with a clumsy, timid foot.

Family Album

In memory of Daniel Alegría R,
who fought for the Nicaraguan people

"It would be that madman, Uncle Sergio," Ximena murmured as she replaced the receiver. It was two in the morning in Paris and the heat was suffocating. No, she wouldn't wake Marcel up now.

Shuffling along in her slippers, she went into the kitchen to make a cup of tea.

Sergio and his obsessions. It had begun with the fingernails and locks of hair. He had stored them carefully in a plastic bag and every three months he had placed the bag inside the coffin that Mariano, the carpenter down the road, had made to measure, and which he stored under his four-poster bed.

Where on earth did Uncle Sergio get his obsessions from?

When the water was boiling, Ximena poured it over a Lipton teabag and sat down on the little bench she used as a stepladder.

Once a year, on the feast of St. Antony of Padua, Sergio celebrated his own funeral. He pulled the coffin out from underneath the bed and placed the little bag of nails and hair in the bedroom closet. The coffin, made of mahogany and lined with white satin, was meticulously polished and stood in the center of the room, with four giant candles keeping watch at the corners.

The funeral had become a tradition in Santa Ana. Precisely at noon all his old friends gathered at the house and he served them a grand dinner with chicken timbale and wines selected from his cellar. Women were not allowed. On these occasions, Lupe took refuge in one of her sisters' houses, so that she did not have to witness her husband's display of madness.

When the clock in the corridor struck three and the cigars and brandy were finished and the cheeks of the guests were flushed with heat and alcohol, all the men retired to the drawing room. There they laid aside the bouquets of purple and white lilies and the crown of white carnations and margueritas that spelled "Sergio, you will always live on in memory," and assisted him – all decked out in his black suit, black tie and even the black shoes that only emerged on such occasions — to climb into the coffin.

Four bottles of beer and some ham and cheese sandwiches were then put into the coffin with great solemnity and it was sealed up, although the lid was perforated with air-holes to allow Uncle Sergio to keep breathing.

Six of his most intimate friends then lifted the bier on to their shoulders and, with appropriately mournful expressions, carried the coffin to the hearse waiting at the door.

When they reached the cemetery these friends lifted the bier to their shoulders again and carried it to the mausoleum, which had been prepared to receive it.

They sealed up the entrance, and there Uncle Sergio remained until evening, when the gravedigger would come and open it up again and so release him.

Ximena shook her head and went over to the sink with her empty cup. What can be happening to Uncle Sergio in the other Santa Ana? she pondered.

She wasn't tired but returned to bed anyway. Marcel was sleeping soundly. How well that two-week holiday in Brittany had gone for him. My father's bones . . . what would Sergio be doing with them? Why hasn't Roberto written? I must get some sleep, she said to herself, tossing about and shutting her eyes firmly. What can be happening to Sergio in the other Santa Ana?

Was it he who did Mamita Rosa out of her estate? She could hear Chus Ascat's voice quite clearly: "If you want to know the truth, it won't be long now before Uncle Sergio turns up here. Part of his body is already here with us. It's frightening to look at. The left leg is sound, but all the rest is covered with the hairs he spent a lifetime saving, and his nails have turned into hooves. Poor don Sergio, although he deserves every last bit of it in return for his meanness. Do you know what his punishment is? To pick coffee beans. Thousands and thousands of coffee beans, without help from anyone. To pick a whole harvest for all the workers he mistreated. It's a shame to hear him moaning, but he's got his just desserts, and he's getting hairier and hairier every day."

"How can you say such a thing? He's at home issuing orders just as usual."

"Over here it's a different matter. You still haven't understood."

Ximena opened her eyes and peered into the darkness. She'd learned a lot from Chus, things that Indians keep hidden from whites: a song to attract birds, another to keep the dead away.

"How do you say *child* in Nahuatl, Chus?"

"Cunet."

"And *bed?*"

"Tapexco, but take care." She looked deep into her eyes. "If I discover you've been repeating the things I tell you, you'll soon feel my curse upon you. Nahuatl is a sacred language and every Indian has a secret name nobody else is allowed to know. You have one, too. One of these days I'll tell it to you, along with that of my dead daughter, may she rest in peace. You drank my milk, and it's right you should know, but don't repeat it to anyone, not even your mother, if you don't want to risk losing your immortal soul."

Ximena was twelve when Chus had suddenly died of tetanus, and she still hadn't learned her secret name. For days she was inconsolable, until one night Chus appeared to her in a dream.

"Stop crying now," she told her, "mourning keeps me earthbound, and I have so much to do in the other Santa Ana."

Ximena stopped crying. She liked talking with Chus when, as now, the light was out and she was waiting to fall asleep. They conversed in low voices so no one could hear them. Each time Ximena had a problem, Chus advised her what course to follow and she was always right.

She learned a lot about the other Santa Ana. Two weeks after Felipe Cuevas was hacked to death on the way to his mother's house, Ximena asked after him.

Chus gazed at her in silence.

"Why don't you want to tell me, Chus?"

"Your mother wouldn't like it."

"I never tell Mommy a thing you say to me. Don't you remember our pact? Never a word to anyone."

Chus laughed to herself silently.

"You liked him, didn't you?"

"He used to take me for rides on his motorbike."

"And he always carried a gun."

"Only to defend himself."

"And to shoot at any poor kids who climbed up his jocote tree when they were hungry and looking for fruit. He potted them as though they were vultures. He'd laugh aloud when one of them fell. Now it's a different matter. He's been turned into a huge vulture and can only eat rotting carrion. The children he killed throw stones and make fun of him: they won't leave him in peace to enjoy his feast."

"And Daddy, Chus, how's he?"

She tossed again in her bed. She had to sleep. At least she was still on vacation. A few moments later, or perhaps closer to a couple of hours, she awoke again thinking about Mamita Rosa.

Mamita Rosa was nearly ninety when she died. Ximena's father, a doctor, had warned them she couldn't hold on much longer. She was dying of a stomach cancer, not the ulcer she'd been told about.

Ximena had grabbed a moment when no one was around to slip down the corridor to her bedroom, separated by a screen from the corner where Aunt Tula was sleeping. She knelt breathlessly at her bedside, and, taking the old lady's withered and yellow hand in her own, whispered: "Mamita Rosa, you're a saint, and now that you're about to die I want you to ask the Virgin to grant me three wishes."

"What are they?"

"That I get away from here, that I love my husband very much, and that I become a writer."

"I'll ask for the first two, but not for the last. I don't like the way poets live."

"But Mamita Rosa . . ."

At this point, Lidia had entered the room, smiling and asking, "How's my old lady?" Ximena scrambled to her feet in embarrassment and stood watching as Lidia arranged the pillows.

"Can I get you something?" Lidia had solicitously inquired, and Ximena felt a pang of guilt, because instead of asking the old lady — on her deathbed, no less — what she could do for her, she'd come in search of miracles.

"Yes," replied Mamita Rosa, her eyes lighting up. "What I'd like most in the world is a bunch of red and white gladioli."

Just then Sergio's wife had appeared. Ximena detested her for being a pedant who wrote incoherent newspaper articles saying there should be laws to prevent illegitimate children from inheriting, as this was an affront to religion and morality.

"What religion and what drivel," her father had said. "The word for that is downright meanness."

Uncle Sergio had loads of illegitimate children who worked as peons on his estates, and Lupe was terrified they might possibly diminish her own two sons' inheritance. She'd undertaken to visit Mamita Rosa once a week and never missed a Wednesday. On this occasion Aunt Tula was closeted in her corner, because Lupe unfailingly managed to drop some nasty remark — just because Aunt Tula liked a swig of wine before going to bed. The poor old thing, as if it was her fault. She and Julio had inherited the habit from their great-grandfather, who'd get drunk and revert to talking about his ancestor, the pirate who had repeatedly crossed the Atlantic in search of pearls and gold ingots and mother-of-pearl and magic seaweed. Still, the whole family had been ashamed of him, most of all Aunt Petronila, because, having left the priesthood, he went and got himself married, on three consecutive occasions, in Cuba, Guatemala and Argentina, and no one could work out which really was his legitimate family.

Julio had died of tuberculosis from having drunk so much hooch. He was the artist of the family, making wood carvings and even a violin which he used to serenade girls, and they all fell for him because he was tall and red-cheeked and healthy and truly handsome. Only he wasn't prepared to sacrifice his freedom to anyone.

Uncle Sergio and Aunt Petronila stopped talking to him they were so ashamed, and the same went for Aunt Tula. They said God was punishing them for their sins, that this was why they were poor, and the two old misers never noticed that Mamita Rosa, saint that she was, was equally poor, nor that Aunt Petronila, who lived in Ahuachapan with her bald, wealthy husband with his gold watch-chain, hardly offered them more than fruit jelly on the rare occasions when they went to visit her, and never parted with money because they complained that Aunt Tula would only drink it and they weren't in the business of fostering vices, may God spare them from anything of the sort.

Poor little Aunt Tula, in the end she became so poor she was reduced to drinking Tic-Tac, almost pure alcohol.

Ximena, partly because she felt sorry for having wanted to take advantage of Mamita Rosa's saintliness, and partly to avoid the new visitor, asked Lidia if she could go along with her to buy the flowers.

There was an abundance of yellow and white gladioli, but no red ones to be found anywhere. Poor Aunt Lidia, who was fat and had bunions and was beginning to weary of her mother's caprices, told Ximena that she'd have to be satisfied with pink rather than red gladioli, that it was all the same anyway. But Ximena resisted firmly:

"*Red* and white were what she asked for, Aunt Lidia. For all we know, this may be her final request."

Finally they found them at a flower stall hidden between a salt-pork shop and one selling live iguanas.

They got home nearly an hour later, with a large bunch of red and white gladioli.

Mamita Rosa was by herself once more. She raised herself up with difficulty and held out her arms in their white cambric sleeves, her thin wrists protruding from the embroidered cuffs. She took the bouquet in her hands and clutched it to her sunken chest. She touched the satiny petals with trembling fingers and murmured: "How pretty they are, and how fresh."

"I'll fetch a vase," offered Ximena.

"No, no," Mamita Rosa replied. "I want them here under my legs."

Lidia pretended not to understand, but Mamita Rosa insisted: "Yes, here under my legs."

Lidia and Ximena exchanged quizzical looks, as Mamita Rosa sank back in her pillows, then parted the sheets.

"Like this," and a smile appeared on her withered lips, "now I can die in peace."

She shut her eyes a moment, and reopened them to say: "I've always wanted to pee on a bunch of gladioli."

A week later Mamita Rosa died and Sergio fumigated the house the next day, to have it ready for renting as soon as possible.

Next it had been his left leg. The gangrene had spread and the leg had to be amputated above the knee. Uncle Sergio was inconsolable at the news for days. He went to Houston to seek the opinion of consultants there and when they confirmed that his leg couldn't be saved he came back to Santa Ana in order to have his old friend and trusted surgeon, Doctor Solorzano, perform the operation.

A week prior to being admitted to the hospital, he summoned Mariano, the carpenter, and ordered a coffin measuring 35 inches long by 8 wide. He issued instructions that the amputated leg should be stored in the freezer he'd bought a few years previously in New Orleans, in which he kept his Maine lobsters, half a slaughtered cow and a variety of patés and sausage.

A few days after emerging from the private clinic and before having his artificial leg fitted — it was endowed with a phenomenal assortment of electronic pistons and gadgets — he invited his cronies over for a meal and gave them a talk on General Santa Ana, hero of the Alamo. He also made passing mention of General Obregón, who had kept his hand pickled in alcohol.

After the dessert had been cleared away, his nurse pushed him into the drawing room in his wheelchair, opened the double doors with a grand and solemn air, and wheeled Uncle Sergio to the head of the little coffin encircled with candles.

Uncle Sergio waved his friends to follow him in and when they were all gathered together he told the nurse to raise the lid.

The nurse ceremoniously opened the box and the guests gazed in stunned disbelief at a kind of sealed aquarium, in which Sergio's leg floated in a dun-colored liquid.

"Who among you can tell me the nature of the fluid preserving my leg?" he asked with a jovial smile.

Total silence.

"Nothing less than Napoleon brandy," he enthused, and his friends applauded and congratulated him on the ingenuity of his idea.

"What time is it?" asked Marcel, stretching.

"Barely seven o'clock. You can still sleep a while longer."

Marcel sat up in bed and stared into space.

"Guess who called last night?" asked Ximena.

"Who?" Marcel's voice was thick with sleep.

"Trinidad. I was going to wake you but you were sleeping so soundly that I couldn't bring myself to."

"Thank goodness. Anything important?"

"For me it was," Ximena was buttoning her flowered housecoat. "Just think, they've disinterred Daddy's bones."

"What on earth for?"

"How would I know! Another of mad Uncle Sergio's whims. He claims that the mausoleum is designated only for the Alvarado family, and that Daddy was a Rodriguez, not an Alvarado."

"What utter stupidity," grumbled Marcel as he pulled on a sock. "And what on earth are they going to do with your father's bones?"

"I haven't the faintest idea."

"Decidedly macabre, your family. How long is it since your father died?"

"Twelve years," replied Ximena absent-mindedly.

"Twelve years. The flesh would have rotted away and only the skeleton would be left, a few bare white bones. What was the name of the classical sites where corpses were left for seven years before being moved to the mausoleum? Rotting rooms, of course."

She felt a shiver run up her spine as she remembered the first time she visited the Escorial. Marcel and she standing in front of the rotting room somewhere in the Escorial's murky corridors, as she thought of the horrible processions of kings, queens and infantas who down the centuries had passed through those very doors, simply in order to rot away.

"What's up?" Marcel was looking at her.

"Nothing," she lied. "I'll go and make your breakfast."

While she prepared coffee and toast she retreated into her private world, a world in which Marcel figured only as a ghost while her thoughts, memories and Chus Ascat were as real as flesh and blood. And bone. Her father's bones. Did her mother know?

Once Marcel had left the apartment, Ximena returned to the bedroom to lie down for a while, but found it impossible to sleep. She dressed, made the bed, and decided to listen to some music.

She put the Solentiname Mass Armando had given her on the record player, sat down on the sofa and lit a cigarette.

Aunt Petronila — who would have thought it? — died long before Aunt Tula. They had to bring her all the way to Santa Ana to be interred in the Alvarado mausoleum.

"If only I'd known, I wouldn't have brought you along," Mommy gazed at me remorsefully.

"We all believed she'd only fainted," explained the maid, "but it was her heart. By the time the doctor arrived, she was gasping her last."

"Her last wish was to be buried in Santa Ana," said her husband, without shedding a tear.

Nor did her children cry, nor the maid, nobody. Everything happened so suddenly they were more stunned than sad.

My father offered to take the corpse away, but the route lay past a police station and carrying corpses around is against the law. Mommy suggested putting Aunt Petronila in the rear seat, between the two of us, but to hurry up before rigor mortis set in. Her husband knotted a blue silk scarf under her chin so her jaw wouldn't drop open, and if the police asked any questions we were to say that she was very ill, with a terrible toothache, and since Daddy was a doctor that everyone knew, they'd be bound to let us through. We got into the car, me already dead with terror, Aunt Petronila wedged between Mommy and me. It had been raining, road conditions were terrible, and Daddy was on edge. The car rocked from side to side and Aunt Petronila swayed in rhythm, and although Mommy tried to hang on to her, it was impossible. Her head fell against my shoulder, I shifted position and it was left dangling. It was horrific to see her like that, with her blue silk head scarf and her mouth half open. Before reaching the police station, Mommy pulled Aunt Petronila against her shoulder. "Poor old lady," the policeman said, "what's wrong?"

"Such a bad toothache she can't even see straight," Daddy lied.

And so we went on, jolting up and down like the oxenless cart that creaks at night through lonely village streets, the oxenless cart that frightens sleepless children with the moans of the dead it's carrying — what was Uncle Sergio going to do with Daddy's bones? — the cart with no oxen rattling its cargo of bones, and when we reached Santa Ana we took her to Uncle Sergio's house and got her carefully out of the car. All the neighbors were in the picture by now and all came to peer, and with help from Daddy and her husband — who'd arrived earlier — and at Uncle Sergio's insistence, she was laid out in his bed while he flapped about her like a bird of ill omen. Aunt Petronila was beginning to go rigid, and despite the blue silk scarf her mouth was hanging half open.

"What's the matter with me?" Ximena shifted uncomfortably on the sofa, "I haven't even smoked a joint. Better if I do something."

She hauled out the dirty linen and put it into the washer. The doorbell rang. She frowned. Who could it be this early? It rang again, three times. She turned on the washer while her visitor insistently rapped with his knuckles.

Madman or thief? The papers were full of hair-raising stories at the moment.

"Who is it?" she asked, before opening the door.

"It's me, Armando."

She unhooked the security chain, opened the door, and a tall scarecrow lifted her up in the air, set her down on the ground, shook a newspaper in her face and asked:

"Have you seen the news?"

"No. Something wrong?"

"Just the opposite, something wonderful. The Sandinistas have seized the National Palace in Managua. They've taken over a thousand hostages. See, read for yourself."

Ximena rapidly looked through the front-page story. There were few details.

"The Sandinista National Liberation Front, the FSLN," she murmured, "you were working with them, weren't you?"

Armando nodded.

"At last we're on our way, Ximena, and still this is only the beginning. The Vampire's days are numbered."

"I really hope so." She handed him back his paper. "Let's go to the kitchen and have a coffee."

"A quick one, then, I've got to go to *Le Figaro*. I've got a friend there who'll let me look at the bulletins as they come in."

Armando was a cousin on her father's side, the Nicaraguan branch of the family.

As she measured out the spoonfuls of coffee, Ximena remembered the day her cousin first appeared in her doorway, coughing and cadaverously thin, his nerves shot by prison and torture, and that look in his eyes, the furtive yet watchful look of the refugee. Now he was nervously pacing up and down. Still thin, but with his health and self-confidence restored.

"Sit down and tell me all about it," said Ximena, settling into the chair facing him.

"I'd just phoned my friend on *Le Figaro* and he said that the guerrilla movement has demanded release and safe conduct abroad for over a hundred political prisoners. They've also demanded ten million dollars and a plane on which to leave the country along with the prisoners. As yet, still no answer from Somoza."

"Do you think they'll get what they want?"

"I think they might. They've got that bastard's back to the wall. His National Guard can't enter the Palace without there being a full-scale massacre of all the deputies and hundreds of others. He's even got a couple members of his family holed up in there. If he doesn't agree to the FSLN's demands, they'll be the first to disappear from the scene."

He lit a cigarette, then vehemently shook the match out.

"The Rigoberto Lopez Perez commando!" he suddenly exclaimed. "You know who he was, don't you?"

"Of course. Daddy knew him. He killed the older Somoza, didn't he?"

"That's right. A suicide mission. Twenty-seven bullets in his body, but the old dictator died despite a whole posse of surgeons despatched to his aid by the gringos. The sad part is that we were still naive in those days. His assassination didn't change a thing. That dynasty was too firmly entrenched. Now it's another story, you mark my words. The FSLN is attacking the system at its very roots."

"Armando," Ximena interrupted his flow, "do you think Mario is in the Palace?"

Armando hesitated.

"I've been wondering about that ever since I saw today's paper. Mario is an intelligent lad, audacious and with steady nerves. Hopefully, he's in there with them."

Ximena got up and took two cups and the sugar-bowl off the shelf.

"How long has he been in the guerrilla movement?" she asked.

"Nearly seven months. He took part in the Masaya uprising in February, after Chamorro was assassinated — do you remember? He must have had at least six months' training and probably some combat experience. It's possible they selected him for this."

Ximena sighed as she recalled Nicaragua's bloodstained history: her great-uncle Zeledón, her father fighting alongside him and later alongside Sandino, Armando in prison for three years. And now Mario.

"Will we ever have peace?" she asked as she carried in the tray.

"Only when the Vampire drops dead, but *this*," he struck the table with his newspaper, "is the first nail in his coffin."

"And how much blood will be spilled before that happens?"

"Rivers of blood, Ximena. The Vampire won't give up easily, but the battle's won. Every repressive act by Somoza from now on will swell the ranks of the FSLN."

"You're a great optimist, Armando. What can a few ill-armed kids do against a National Guard equipped with sub-machineguns and tanks, helicopters and planes? Thousands of young men are going to die, only to have Yankee Marines land on our soil once again."

"Thousands of Nicaraguans have died unnecessarily since the Somoza dynasty took power. But they are the silent dead, Ximena, does that make it easier for you to forget them? That's the other side of the coin, and we're so used to looking at it, it's become invisible. We have to fight on until we win."

"But Washington will never allow that to happen," protested Ximena, "they're convinced that any revolutionary movement is by definition Communist."

"Let them think what they like," Armando shrugged, "the first step is to rid ourselves of the Somoza clan, and if the gringos then want to send in the Marines, let them try. They'll find the world has changed since 1912, particularly if you take Cuba and Vietnam into account. If they want to occupy the country, not only will the entire Nicaraguan people join the FSLN, but so will the rest of Latin America: around 250 million people will have to decide whether they want a free continent or whether they want to carry on under orders from the White House and the Pentagon."

Hopelessly overexcited, Ximena decided, as Armando continued gushing, waving his arms around for emphasis.

"The stink from what's going on in Nicaragua," he added, holding out his cup for more coffee, "will make the whole world want to throw up."

"The stench of the rotting room," murmured Ximena.

Armando's words reminded her of her own obsession, and she stopped listening for a few moments. How selfish I am, she suddenly rebuked herself, Mario is probably in the National Palace ready to die in the next few hours, and here I am preoccupied with what will become of Daddy's bones, and him dead for twelve years.

"Do you know what?" she asked, edging into the first pause, "*I* wouldn't even recognize Mario from a photograph."

"I don't believe it," Armando got up.

"What, are you off?"

"Yes. I've got to meet a Nicaraguan friend in a few minutes. Can you lend me your radio? I'll look after it."

"Of course," Ximena got up as well, "what a pity you have to leave so soon. Why don't you come to dinner tonight? We could watch the in-depth news report."

"Won't that get on Marcel's nerves?"

"No, but come a bit before he gets home and we can talk first."

Once Armando had left, Ximena went distractedly into the bedroom, sat down mechanically at the dressing-table and began brushing the snarls out of her hair.

"How are babies born?" she heard herself ask, looking at her reflection in the mirror.

Chus was sitting on a stool, braiding Ximena's hair in front of the bathroom mirror.

"They come from the other Santa Ana."

"I know that, but who brings them?"

"That depends. Rich people claim their children from the cemetery, poor children wait for parents in the market."

Ximena sat still in silence.

"And where was I brought from?" she asked after a pause.

Chus stopped braiding, sat Ximena on her knees and gave her a kiss.

"I'd say that despite coming from a wealthy family, they found you in the market."

"No Chus, be serious," Ximena wriggled impatiently in her nanny's arms, "I want you to tell me how babies are born."

"We'd better hurry," Chus planted her firmly back on the floor. "You'll be late for school."

"Okay, but answer me," the girl persisted.

"When a wealthy girl gets married," Chus resumed plaiting Ximena's hair, "she has to wait for nine months, and sometimes even more than a year, to go and collect her baby. She goes to the cemetery with her husband, to his family mausoleum, and there they find it all wrapped up in a soft shawl. Before picking it up, they both kneel down to thank God, and then take their bundle home. The only disadvantage is that they have to take whatever they're given. Sometimes they're lucky and everything turns out fine, but occasionally the baby turns out knock-kneed and ugly, as happened with Uncle Sergio's son."

"And do the poor children also arrive from the other Santa Ana?" Ximena inquired.

"Yes, but that's another matter." Chus tied a pink bow into the first braid. "There are so many of them that they all have to be left in the market."

"Who brings them to market?"

"God help me, how you do go on this morning, I think it must be the *cadejo*."*

"The white or the black one?"

"The white one of course. The black one brings bad luck, the only good he does is to protect poor drunks stumbling around in the night. Everyone knows that the white one likes children and I imagine he must carry them in his jaws all the way from the other Santa Ana, making sure not to hurt them, and he deposits them at midnight in the market. That's where the mothers go to buy them."

"To buy them?" Ximena was surprised.

"That's what I said. Poor women like me hardly ever marry but some day, without knowing why or how, our bellies begin to ache and it's definitely not the same as indigestion, so we know that's the sign that the child's on its way, and we run to the market to look. The trouble is that there are so many it can be difficult to be sure which is your own."

"And what if the mother made a mistake?" Ximena asked, terrified.

"That hardly ever happens," Chus burst out laughing, "women always have a sense for the right one. What does sometimes happen is that two women quarrel over the one with the largest eyes, or who for some reason — no one knows how — turns out blue-eyed, or even over the chubbiest."

"And what happens to the ugly or deformed ones?"

"May God give me patience with this little girl. A mother knows in her heart which is her own and she takes it away wrapped in her shawl. Sometimes those are the ones who turn out best."

* *Cadejo*: spirit of a native Central American dog, bringing good or bad luck, depending on the color.

"And Daddy, Chus, how's he?" Ximena overheard herself asking, but no one answered.

Off again, fantasizing as usual, she told herself angrily. I'll go and take a shower while the chicken is cooking.

"Hello," said Marcel, planting a kiss on her neck, "sorry I'm late, but there's a whole backlog of work."

"Doesn't matter," she reassured him, returning the kiss, "we've still got time for a quick drink. I'll turn down the flame on the stove."

Marcel took the ice cubes from the freezer, put them in glasses and began to pour Ricard over them.

"Make mine a large one," Ximena requested, "I really need a drink."

"What's up?" Marcel asked, and she watched him sit down in the chair Armando had vacated.

"Nothing, this whole business of my dad's bones has really put me on edge."

"Do stop thinking about it. In the final analysis, it doesn't matter much where our old bones come to rest."

"I know," Ximena sounded distracted, "that's not what worries me, it's the petty-mindedness of all those people. Why has it taken me until now to realize?"

"It's easier that way."

"The whole incident has jogged my memory and ever since last night the only thing I can think of is my blessed family. On the same subject, do you know who was here today?"

"Who?"

"Armando. He's obsessed with what's going on in Nicaragua. Haven't you seen the newspapers?"

"Yes," Marcel sounded flatly uninterested, "crazy kids, no good can come of it. Or perhaps it will, and Somoza will harden his line even more."

Ximena kept quiet. Few French people seemed able to understand the problems of Latin America. Too Cartesian, too self-satisfied with their own history.

"I invited him to dinner," she announced after a while, "so we can see the news reports together. He doesn't have a television."

"I don't know if I can make it," Marcel sighed again. "With this heat and the backlog of work I finish the day completely wiped out. And I must say, too, that your cousin with all his eloquent speeches, his revolutionary romanticism and his lack of political realism, gets on my nerves."

Ximena gulped the last of her drink and got up to take a look at the rice.

"Do you know," she sat down at the table again, "my family divides into people who take and people who give?"

Marcel broke into laughter.

"Did I ever tell you about Aunt Clotilde?"

"I don't think so."

"She was a wonderful woman, good, intelligent, beautiful, very much like my mother. She got married to a rich man, Alfredo, whom everyone called Raw Silk because that was the only fabric he'd wear."

"What?" Marcel was astonished.

"That's right. He had at least twenty-four identical suits. He was a gambler, and soon after getting married he lost his whole inheritance. When he died, he left my poor aunt without a penny and only the house in which she was raising their four children. The youngest was less than a year old at the time."

"It's phenomenal that you can remember all these family histories you never even lived through."

"I've always loved having people tell me stories, Mamita Rosa and my mother were great at it."

"And you're great at making rice," rejoined Marcel, regretting his outburst against Armando. "It's turned out exquisitely."

"You sweetheart," said Ximena, feeling like Scheherazade, "do you really enjoy my stories?"

"Enormously," Marcel lied. "I love you to tell me stories."

"Okay then, Uncle Alfredo . . ."

"Raw Silk," interrupted Marcel.

Ximena nodded.

"He'd scarcely been dead five days when one afternoon, following the novena, his sister told Aunt Clotilde she wanted to talk to her about something very important. Aunt Clotilde felt her heart skip a beat. Her sister-in-law was a wealthy woman and she thought she must be about to offer her something to help with the children. The two of them perched on wicker chairs in the little drawing-room."

"At least you've invented the setting, haven't you?"

"Of course not. Mamita Rosa gave me very precise details of everything."

"All right then. Go on."

"Aunt Clotilde served her sister-in-law coffee and the cheese buns that Conchita always baked — she's famous for them all over Santa Ana — then sent the girl off to the market to buy the best sugar buns. 'Ay, Cloti,' the old woman began, 'I don't know how to tell you this, but I'm sure you'll understand. My poor brother, may God rest his soul, was so muddle-headed he left behind a pile of debts all over the place.'

'I know,' my aunt answered, 'but Francisco and Miguel will soon start work and I pray to God He'll take care of paying them.'

'They're only kids,' her sister-in-law replied, her jowls stuffed with cheese bun, 'I hope you won't be taking them out of school.'

'I've got no choice,' my aunt replied.

'You won't like what I'm about to tell you,' the old woman went on, 'but debts are debts.'"

"A little more rice please," interjected Marcel.

"My aunt looked at her uncomprehendingly." Ximena passed him the dish of rice.

"'You know how Alfredo liked gambling,' the old woman's double chin was wobbling, 'and that was his downfall. Didn't I ever tell you about the debt he's owed to me since we were both youngsters?'

'No.'

'Well, I've brought along the paper signed in his own hand. Here.'

Aunt Clotilde began reading with difficulty. The paper read: 'I, Alfredo Saenz, declare that I have sold my house, 36, Tercera Avenida Norte, to my sister Eduviges . . .'"

"Edu-who?" asked Marcel.

"Eduviges. Even her name was hideous . . . 'and have received from her the sum agreed and my sister has graciously consented to let me live in it until the day I die'," concluded Ximena in a pompous voice.

"'Signed Alfredo Saenz, Santa Ana, on January 14, 1914.'

'He never mentioned any of this,' Aunt Clotilde's voice was breaking, 'but I imagine, Eduviges, that this piece of paper is worthless, the two of you were still only children.'

'A debt is a debt,' repeated the old woman, crossing and uncrossing her legs: she was hardly able to manage it, they were so short.

'How much did you give him for it?'

'I can't remember any more. I think it was five thousand *colones,* which was a capital sum in those days.'

'The house is worth far more than that, and it's all the children and I possess.'

'I'm sorry, Clotilde, but since you're not in a position to pay, I want you to be out in three months. Otherwise we'll have to take it to court and that's such a disagreeable business within families.'

My aunt got up and went to her room in tears. At the end of three months, a friend lent her a house."

"Your aunt was pretty silly," Marcel said, "any lawyer could have settled it. Didn't your Uncle Sergio help her?"

"You're joking. He said it was nothing to do with him, that Eduviges and his wife Lupe were like sisters and that in any case Alfredo was no child when he signed this, that he was eighteen years old. Nobody came to my poor aunt's assistance apart from her saints."

"And how did her saints help her?"

"I know it'll all seem daft to you, you're an out-and-out Gallic non-believer," Ximena smiled. "Mamita Rosa, who never told a lie in her life, told me the story lots of times. She said that one evening Aunt Clotilde couldn't find anything at all to give her children to eat. There was nothing in the house, and a big storm was brewing. My aunt knelt down in the living room — which was also the dining room and bedroom — before an ancient wooden crucifix which had belonged to Alfredo's grandfather. She was at prayer when the door flew open and a great blast of wind swept in. When she got up to close the door she found, there in the middle of the room, a one hundred *colon* note. Can you imagine that?"

"Sheer coincidence," said Marcel, "it fell from the pocket of some old drunk into the street where the wind picked it up."

"I don't believe in coincidences," replied Ximena. "But we'll discuss that some other time. On another occasion, at about six in the morning, my aunt was gazing out of the window wondering what she could find the children for breakfast, when she saw a boy she'd never seen before walking down the street, selling milk and bread. In Santa Ana the baker never supplies milk nor the milkman bread."

"A law against it?" asked Marcel.

"No but that's the way things are. Besides, as I told you, my aunt had never seen the boy in her life and was surprised when he greeted her affectionately: 'How are you, Miss Cloti, how much do you want me to leave you today?'

'I haven't a penny to give you,' said my aunt.

'It doesn't matter, you can pay me later,' said the boy. 'See, I'll leave you two bottles of milk, a French loaf and two cheese buns.'

The boy never reappeared," Ximena said in a low voice, "isn't that weird?"

"Yes," Marcel admitted. "Did you know your aunt?"

"Yes, but I can scarcely remember her. She died of tuberculosis when I was barely ten years old."

"Mamita Rosa lived off flowers," she went on to herself, "and Aunt Clotilde off miracles."

She looked down at her plate and noticed she hadn't taken a single bite.

The minute Marcel left for the office she ran to the telephone and asked to be put through to Santa Ana. It was eight in the morning in El Salvador, and Roberto would be getting up. While she waited for the connection, she began worrying about what she could tell Marcel. He always scrutinized the monthly bills closely through his tortoiseshell glasses, asking implacably the why and wherefore of that particular call on August 23 or whatever. Her heart would thump fiercely as she listened to his voice: "We can't go on like this; I'm fed up with your extravagance, when are you going to learn to economize so that we can finally buy a place of our own?"

Ximena was on the point of canceling the call.

No, I can't, it's important to me. I'll put in extra hours at the school, I'll manage to find other ways to save.

She had to wait nearly an hour to be put through. She cleared the table, washed the dishes and smoked at least five cigarettes.

At long last the operator told her that her call was connected. The line was poor, but it was definitely Roberto's voice.

"Hello, it's me, Ximena."

"Hello. Something up?"

"No, what could be up over here? Trinidad rang last night to tell me the latest about Uncle Sergio."

"He's an old fool; you can't expect any better of him."

"But what will happen to Daddy's bones?"

"I'm making arrangements to build a mausoleum. Didn't you get my letter?"

"No."

"Strange, I sent it with Trinidad's. Uncle Sergio said he's never setting foot in her house again."

"I don't believe you. Is Mommy aware of what's going on?"

"No, you're joking. And you'd better come soon if you want her to recognize you."

The line went dead. Ximena went on trying, "Hello, hello," but that was it.

She replaced the receiver, lit another cigarette and lay down on the sofa again. She realized that she felt sleepy.

How frustrating phone calls are. I know about as much as I did before. Poor Mommy, maybe it's just as well the world passes her by now. I should go and see her and stay for Christmas. It wouldn't surprise me in the least if in a fit of rage Uncle Sergio had Daddy's bones thrown into the river. Anyway, when all's said and done, the bones aren't the person. The best choice is cremation, with the ashes used to fertilize a garden. I'd love to fertilize a purple bougainvillea like the one we had at home. It's odd how Chus never mentions Daddy. Roberto's right: what else could one expect of Uncle Sergio?

After Grandfather's death, Sergio came to Mamita Rosa's house to discuss the debts the old man had left behind.

"Don't fuss, Mother," he told her, "I think I can help you."

"God bless you, son," Mamita Rosa replied, "but it's not right that you should have to look after both Tula and me. You've got a wife and children. Perhaps we can mortgage the coffee plantation."

"Here you are," said Sergio, handing her two bills of 100 *colones*. "This should get you through the next few days. My wife has a house you and Tula should move into as soon as possible, so you won't have to pay rent."

"You're a wonderful son," said Mamita Rosa, grasping his hands.

"Don't be silly. All you have to do is to sign this piece of paper that gives me your full permission to fight your battles with the lawyers and the bankers."

"Praise be to God," replied Mamita Rosa and signed the paper. She got up and kissed Sergio, saying: "Whatever would we have done without you?"

A week later Mamita Rosa and Aunt Tula moved to the house belonging to Sergio's wife. It was much smaller than their previous one, but they decided that didn't matter. The

93

dining room was in the kitchen, it had two minuscule bedrooms and a few feet of ground covered in weeds.

"You could have fun with this garden," Sergio announced.

"How good you are, son. You'll see how soon we get the weeds cleared. I'll plant flowers of all colors, and shrubs that won't spread too much. A gardenia would be lovely, wouldn't it?"

Mamita Rosa arranged the garden so beautifully that two years later Sergio rented the house and moved his mother and aunt to an even smaller one with only two flowerbeds to save them the trouble of doing so much gardening.

The telephone rang. Ximena had been asleep and woke with a start.

"It all went as it should, Ximena, everything worked out," she heard Armando's voice pouring out the news. "Somoza had to give in. He'll release the political prisoners and has guaranteed them safe conduct along with the boys of the FSLN, so they can get out of the country. What do you think of that?"

"Fantastic, Armando. When are they leaving?"

"No one knows yet. The latest bulletin has just come into *Le Figaro*. Tonight we'll celebrate. I'll bring champagne."

"How wonderful, this means that Mario is safe."

"That's right. They'll be broadcasting direct by satellite. Don't forget to watch your television."

"Of course not. Come early and we can chat alone without Marcel picking a fight with you."

"Yes, definitely," and Armando hung up.

Ximena consulted her watch. There was still an hour to go until the news. She'd go out and do the shopping right away.

As she set off for the grocery store, a basket on her shoulder, she remembered all the times her father had predicted Somoza's imminent downfall. How happy he'd be now to hear the news. Night after night, hunched over his radio in the corridor of the old house, trying to tune into Radio Costa Rica all through the last crisis, when it seemed the tyrant couldn't possibly hold out. His face lit up with joy, the lamplight shining in his grey hair. Hour after hour over the short-wave radio without showing the least sign of impatience, suddenly summoning us with some fragment of news he'd managed to catch, Daddy reduced to dust, even his eyes, the wide mouth I'd always longed to kiss devoured by worms, reduced to dust. In the end I did kiss them. They were cold. We were alone that night, alone, with only the rain and an enormous Christ, draped in heavy black tulle, as witnesses.

"Did you watch the news?" asked Armando, leaving the leather briefcase that went everywhere with him in a corner of the room.

"Of course. Let me pour us both a large dry Martini. We ought to begin the celebrations."

"What a drag there weren't any close-up photos." Armando was impatient, "It was impossible to make out any features with those kerchiefs tied around their faces."

Ximena appeared with two generous Martinis, gave one to Armando and raised her glass:

> "To Nicaragua, dear sirs,
> To the land of our birth,
> To the most precious flower
> On American earth."

"Do you remember," she asked, "how much our father liked those lines from his 'eponymous Rubén'?" *

"Of course," answered Armando, "how could I forget? He was a great man, and just imagine what he'd be feeling at this moment."

By the time they sat down to the table, Armando and Ximena had consumed three Martinis apiece and their tongues were loosened. Ximena, however, remained sufficiently lucid to avert major discussion on the topic of Nicaragua.

* Rubén Darío: Nicaragua's greatest poet.

Armando went with the flow. Marcel didn't conceal his dislike of violence and guerrilla movements, and neither of the others were willing to sit through any lengthy monologues on the topic of *la gloire de France,* its advanced form of democracy and its wonderful and unique cultural achievements.

Unfortunately, as dessert was being served, Ximena made the mistake of reminding Armando how Uncle Sergio had done Mamita Rosa out of her coffee plantation, forcing her to live out her days in a dark, dank hovel.

This observation unleashed Armando.

"What you fail to understand, Ximena, is that it's not only Uncle Sergio or your Aunt Cloti's sister-in-law who are to blame. Stinginess and avarice aren't the exclusive monopoly of Santa Ana."

"That may be true, but I think it's worse there than elsewhere," rejoined Ximena.

"It's the same story throughout Central America. You're either a latifundista* or a landless peasant. If you don't want to be a victim you have to become a conquistador."

"But you can't turn against your own family," Ximena protested.

"You certainly can. The logic of the market place. The peasants and the workers have been so exploited they've no longer anything to give but their sweat. The ambitious *conquistador* finds himself obliged to strip the trusting, incompetent family 'Indians' of whatever patch of land they may still possess. Cast a glance at the biographies of the richest families in Central America and you'll see how nearly all behaved in the same way."

Marcel swallowed a yawn, and Ximena did her best to give the conversation a different turn, but in vain.

"The successful *conquistador*," Armando continued imperturbably, "not only knows how to steal but also knows how to preserve what he steals, and for this he needs tenacity and a sovereign contempt for his neighbor. In every single Central

* *Latifundista:* major landowner.

96

American country, with the sole exception of Costa Rica, there's the model of revolving dictatorships. Look at the Somozas. After forty-five years in power, the family owns eighty-five percent of the gross national product and thirteen percent of its land. The lushest thirteen percent, it goes without saying."

Marcel took an ostentatious look at his wrist-watch. "I'm sorry I can't stay and have coffee with you, but I've got a lot of work to catch up on."

"What a pity," said Ximena as she watched him walk away.

"Sorry," Armando said, "I completely forgot myself. Me and my missionary zeal."

"It doesn't matter."

"It always happens to me, I forget that words can never carry enough of a charge. Marcel will never understand our problems, unless he goes to Central America and feels them in his own flesh and bones. He has to live with them, until they seem as familiar and unconditionally horrible as the Eiffel Tower."

"How can we liberate ourselves from the Eiffel Tower?" Ximena challenged.

"With dynamite. Or else by educating the public to realize how hideous it really is, until a referendum votes for its destruction. Or by convincing the Gillette company that it's a public menace and should be knocked down and turned into razor blades."

"You're incorrigible!" Ximena burst out laughing.

"It's your attitude that bothers me," Armando's eyes were fixed on her, "you were raised in that sea of misery, and you've erased all trace of it. Since your father was a doctor, naturally things went well for him. You could travel abroad to complete your studies. Then you married a Frenchman and immersed yourself in the placid daily life of the *petit bourgeois,* without troubling yourself further about your own people. Until, that is, the moment when your daft Uncle Sergio decides to remove your father's bones from his mausoleum, something that at the end of the day is entirely meaningless. Don't you ever feel even the least bit uncomfortable? What have you done to help your people? You're very complacent Ximena, your creature comforts are too important to you."

"What would you have me do?" She was on the defensive. "My name isn't Joan of Arc, and even if it was, what good would it do for me to board the next plane out, a dismantled rifle concealed in my suitcase? It'd be about as useful as attacking the Eiffel Tower with a cardboard axe."

"You could show a little more interest. Stop being quite so blasé. Explain the problem to Marcel, talk about it to your friends, raise it as a topic in school. If a larger number of Germans had bothered to concern themselves with Hitler's ravings, perhaps they could have spared the world thirty-six million corpses. Once you understand this, you'll find it a lot easier to figure out how to be useful. That's something we can all be."

"And what are you doing to advance such a noble cause from Paris?"

"Far less than I'd like," conceded Armando, getting out of his chair. "What do you say to our drinking a toast from the bottle I brought along?"

"Fine, but first the coffee," said Ximena, setting off for the kitchen.

The champagne turned out to be a bottle of brandy and Ximena looked at it uneasily. Three dry Martinis, two glasses of wine, and now this. Well, it didn't matter, there was something worth celebrating.

"Tell me, what are you doing?" she insisted.

She put the tray with the coffee cups and the two brandy glasses down on the table in the middle of the room, picked up a cup and sat herself down on the sofa next to Armando.

"I told you, very little." Armando slowly stirred sugar into his coffee. "The boys of the FSLN send me their information bulletins, I translate them into French and do my best to distribute them. Occasionally, through some friend or other, I manage to get something into *Le Monde* or *Le Figaro*. I didn't choose my circumstances, Ximena, they were imposed on me."

"Forgive me." She had never known of this side of Armando's Parisian life. "Now I can see why you have so many journalist friends.

"Mmm," Armando's smile was ironic, "aside from this I spend my time awakening political consciousness in the souls of bored housewives such as yourself. What a grand role, the valiant revolutionary exile in his overcoat and woolen gloves, hunched over a typewriter in some freezing dark attic in the Rue Mouffetard, tapping away with numb fingers until his vision fades and his mind begins to stray. Doesn't it remind you of Lenin when he was in Switzerland writing the editorials for *Iskra?* The only slight difference is that my job consists in addressing envelopes to Parisian ladies containing junk mail about cosmetics."

He swallowed the remainder of his coffee in a gulp and bent down to retrieve his leather briefcase.

"You told me you'd never seen Mario, so I decided to bring this along."

He removed a photo album from the case and put it on his knees. "Why don't you pour us a brandy? My wife went around collecting photos while I was in jail," he took a first sip, "it was the only thing I brought out with me, except for a change of underwear and a raincoat."

He began leafing through the album and stopped at a page somewhere in the middle.

"This is the last picture taken of the whole family. It was taken a few days before I was arrested. Mario was barely thirteen years old."

"How handsome you both are. He looks like Maruca. Did you manage to see them again before leaving for Costa Rica?"

"No, the boys only allowed Maruca to come and see me. She came to a friend's house where we were taken for a few minutes before the truck arrived to take us out. All the better that she actually brought the photo album. It was horrible trying to catch up on three years in those ten minutes. Look here," he was leafing through the pages again, "now he's already a big lad of nineteen. This was taken on his birthday, a month before he joined the guerrillas."

Ximena looked carefully at the photograph of a strong young man, smiling in his football uniform. He had the same wide mouth as all the Rodriguez's, high cheekbones and the rebellious straight hair of his father.

"At that point the baby of the family knew he was off to the guerrillas, but he was keeping it all well under his hat," Armando laughed as he knocked back another swig. "He took up sports to develop his muscles. He didn't say a word to Maruca nor did he put anything in his letters to me. He wasn't able to." He swallowed the rest of his brandy and paused in thought. "Naturally that would have been a breach of security. These separations are so difficult, a youngster changes so much during adolescence. It's been six years since I saw him."

Ximena stared into space, trying to imagine how such a long separation could have sapped both father and son. Armando had certainly become more taciturn, he'd had no alternative but to live on the edge. How good it would be if Maruca came and saw him. Or maybe not. So many experiences they'd been unable to share might come between them until they felt distanced and uncomfortable being together.

"He wrote to me once a month," Armando continued, pouring himself another glass, "his letters were intelligent, but didn't offer any political opinions, he must have been worried about compromising me."

"It's time for the news," said Ximena, "I'll turn the television on."

The two of them settled into the sofa in silence as the screen lit up.

"President Anastasio Somoza," the voice announced, "has conceded to the demands made by a commando group of the Sandinista Front who have been keeping over a thousand people hostage in the Managua National Palace for the last thirty hours. The guerrilla organization demanded the freedom of over a hundred political prisoners and safe conduct out for both the prisoners and themselves."

The two of them watched with concentration as the school bus left the National Palace, inside it the FSLN commando group and their nine hostages.

"At least sixty political prisoners will be set free," continued the newscaster, "to meet up with the guerrillas at the airport, where they'll board a plane for Panama."

The entire route to the airport was crammed with people shouting "Viva!" to the guerrillas, as they waved back from inside the bus.

The program gave way to other international events and Armando got up and switched off the television.

"Sixty prisoners," he said in a sour voice, "the FSLN demanded a hundred political prisoners. I assume you know why they only released sixty, don't you?"

"No. Why?"

"The rest died under torture, of course. The FSLN knew they were already dead. They have their information sources inside the jails. It's a way of highlighting the Vampire's crimes."

"Why do you keep calling him the Vampire?"

"Haven't you heard of Operation Vampire?" asked Armando incredulously. "What we saw tonight on television was the culmination of just one episode in the Somoza family history. Do you remember the uprisings in February after Chamorro's assassination? And the Monimbo massacre?"

Ximena nodded.

"Right, well the FSLN attack on the National Palace is their response to these events. Chamorro was assassinated because the Somozas knew that he was about to publish an article called 'Operation Vampire' in his newspaper, and they weren't going to allow it. It all began immediately after the Managua earthquake in 1972, surely you remember?"

"Yes, now I remember. El Gordo Gomez told me all about it. Somoza sold the blood plasma donated for the wounded back to the United States, didn't he?"

"At twenty dollars a liter. The deal was so good that they began a campaign to get the poor people to donate blood; they got paid a few centavos or nothing at all, and Somoza sent Nicaraguan blood off to the United States. They made another fortune out of that little business."

He knocked back another gulp, and the two sat in silence.

"I knew most of them," Armando took up the thread of the conversation again, "their ghosts people my dreams, or rather my insomnia. I was there as they were taken from their cells, never to return. I could recite all their names."

"And you, how did you escape? You never told me the story."

After two brandies she was starting to feel dizzy, and she curled up against the cushions on the sofa.

"I was picked up with four other comrades. They tortured the lot of us. Rubber truncheons, electric prods, the hood."

"What's the hood?"

"It's a very economical method. They sit you down and tie your arms and legs to the chair. Then they put a plastic bag over your head and tie it tightly around your neck with a thong. It's a form of slow martyrdom, gradual suffocation. Every time you breathe out the plastic bag inflates, and when you breathe in it sticks to your face. Soon you begin to want to thrash around and start lashing out in desperation. One of the boys ended up with a detached retina."

"How horrible!"

"They used to use the submarine, until they decided it was too mucky. The floors got slippery from all the vomit and water. It was the Texan bastard who taught them the hood technique. The gringos perfected it in Vietnam. If you throw up inside it, there's nothing to clean up beyond what's left stuck in your hair. But I'm going off on a tangent," he said, gulping down the remainder of his brandy. "As I was saying, there were five of us, and one sang. No one knows who he was, not even the guy himself."

"What do you mean?"

"Ximena, you can have no idea of what it was like. The psychological tension, the demoralization, the ways they have of driving you mad. After a week of torture you're a piece of shit. And then they inject you with drugs, and you've no memory of anything you've said. None of us owned up to talking, we all genuinely denied the possibility — which we all found equally horrible — but I wonder if any of us could have been absolutely certain. I don't believe it was me, but it could have been, it's always a possibility."

He blinked rapidly, replaced his glass on the table with great care, and suddenly sobbed so fiercely that his whole body shook.

"It could have been me," he repeated, "do you realize what that means?"

He lit a cigarette with trembling hands.

"The damage was done, but we didn't find out until long afterwards. We were left to fester for three years, slowly moldering away, and daily repeating the same question to ourselves. One morning another group of four Sandinistas was brought in. One of them was a big fish, too big to be left to rot in jail. He knew too much about the structure of the organization and that was a serious matter. That night, at around four in the morning, one of the guards opened our door and as we walked out we stumbled over the bodies of the other three night guards that he'd killed. We hadn't heard anything because his pistol had a silencer. He was one of our men, but for three years we'd never suspected a thing. He never said a word to us other than to bark out orders, never gave us a cigarette or a friendly look. Nothing. No one suspected anything about him. You can imagine how useful he was to the FSLN, but they decided to blow his cover to keep our 'big fish' from falling into the hands of the torturers."

"No one saw you get out of there?"

"No, no one. They put the new group into one car, us into another. They took us to a house on the outskirts of Managua and an FSLN commander interviewed us one by one. That was when I realized they no longer trusted me."

"How come?"

"The guy interviewing me had a kerchief covering nearly the whole of his face, so that I couldn't recognize him. After a series of questions he informed me I'd have to leave the country at once. It was at this point they told me I could have ten minutes to see my wife. She was waiting for me in another room and handed me a case containing the album."

"And the other four?"

"They took us all to the Costa Rican border. It was the right thing to do. One rotten apple spoils the whole barrel. But that's hard to swallow, Ximena. The moral suffering is the worst. What use was I any more? I'm no use to the guerrilla, nor to my wife, nor to my children. I'm Mr. Nobody, a weak, broken man, perhaps even a traitor."

"Don't be daft, Armando. What's happened is that we've let ourselves drink too much. Let me reheat the coffee."

"Please don't," Armando put out an arm to bar her way, "don't go. Tonight I need to unwind. Do you know it's the first time I've been able to do this?"

He's right, let him talk, Ximena could hear Chus' voice.

"Another brandy?" offered Armando.

"No, I can't handle any more." Ximena settled herself back on the cushions.

"I can. Why on earth should I keep myself sober? I can only talk if I'm at least half-way drunk, and I need to talk. I'm a nobody, Ximena, a nobody. What am I doing over here? The sole difference between Nicaragua and Paris is that my Parisian cell has a window and I spend my entire day writing lists of addresses."

Tell him something amusing, instructed Chus, *there's a dark cloud over his head and if he goes on like this he'll end up contemplating suicide.*

But what can I tell him, Chus? Nothing comes to mind.

"I think it's time to go back," announced Armando.

"What for? So they can take you prisoner again? You're not a boy any more, Armando. At your age the chains weigh more heavily."

Armando said nothing.

"Unless you find yourself a charitable soul like the famous Miss Sofia Amengual, who gave Salvadorean prisoners new chains that were less heavy."

"She was a dreadful old cow," muttered Armando.

"Her only crime was lack of imagination. It was the only thing she could think of doing with all her millions."

"What other option is there for me?" Armando broke in. "It's worse to putrefy here without doing anything useful."

"My father was her family doctor." Ximena ignored him. "After Sofia died, her eldest son came to him for spiritual guidance. He wanted to know what he could do to erase the memories his mother had left behind. Daddy advised him to build a children's hospital, and do you know what they did? They repaired a wing of the San Juan de Dios hospital, donated seventy-five crummy second-hand cots, and put a bronze plaque up over the door that read: "Sofia Amengual Ward"."

"I didn't know any of this," Armando sounded absent-minded, "it was after my time."

"Don Fulgencio was another matter. He was the black sheep of the family, a real old charmer. In order to eat he bred fighting cocks, but every time he had to sell one off it was a major tragedy. The only part of his inheritance he managed to hang on to was an old country house that was so tumbled down he converted it into a hen house. He gave his champion cocks a bedroom apiece and ended up himself on a camp-bed in the kitchen. The old woman who came in to feed the cocks found him dead one day. Of course the family took charge of all the funeral arrangements, a mahogany casket lined with silk, a wake in the home of one of his nephews, heaps of flowers and coronets. Do you know the story of the burial?"

"No." Armando's mind was elsewhere.

"When they put the coffin into the hearse, a scarlet fighting cock appeared from nowhere, and led the cortege all the way to the cemetery."

"Pure imagination," Armando was laughing now.

"I swear before God. Anyone in Santa Ana can tell you."

"Since we're on the subject of corpses, is it true that it took three days for someone to come across Aunt Tula's?"

"Yes."

"She was a delightful woman. I used to see her often during the year I lived at your house. Sometimes I'd bring her a bottle of wine and we'd play cards until it was empty."

"Like Don Fulgencio she was the black sheep, and except for Mommy and Aunt Lidia, hardly anyone visited her. What we gave her to spend on food she wasted on Tic-Tac. Some say she died of cirrhosis, others of malnutrition. The only thing for certain is that they found her after three days – in that Santa Ana heat, can you imagine it? Her dog was there at her feet."

"And no doubt, to maintain appearances, Uncle Sergio organized another grand funeral."

"Quite so. We're a dreadful family."

"I think it's time for the next news." Armando switched the television on again. "Nearly eleven o'clock."

He looks just like Daddy, Ximena thought as he tuned the set, same neck, same slightly hunched back.

You should see how happy the Doctor is now, interpolated Chus. *He frightened me the day he arrived. He looked so dispirited and hardly spoke a word. Those years in exile had done him in.*

He died without returning to Nicaragua, Ximena thought. Not even his bones.

Now you can see how content he is, Chus continued. *His cheeks are ruddy and he rides around on the sorrel mare he brought from Estelí.*

An advertisement for some new furniture cleaning product flashed up. Armando was staring intently at the screen, as though trying to hypnotize it into ending the ads. When at last the news began, he leaned forward, drumming the arm of the sofa with his fingers.

"Now!" Ximena exclaimed as the words MANAGUA AIRPORT: DIRECT BY SATELLITE flashed on to the screen.

A transport plane materialized before their eyes. A school bus stopped to unload its cargo of armed guerrillas at the stairway, and a band of men in uniform began filing in a vigilant line from the bus to the airplane. After the guerrillas came three men in priests' cassocks and another six in civilian clothes. All nine were escorted to the airplane.

"The hostages and the negotiators," whispered Armando.

The line of masked men slowly climbed up into the airplane, so that finally only one was left at the foot of the stairway. He addressed the television reporter. In a single movement, he pulled down the scarf that had covered the lower half of his face and the camera focused on him in close-up.

"Good God!" Armando was up out of his seat, "it's Edén!"

"Who?"

"Edén Pastora.* Commander Cero. I knew him in Costa Rica."

"Shhh. Listen."

"After this, Somoza will fall, he's bound to fall, even if I can't tell you exactly when," Pastora was addressing the interviewer. "The whole intention of our operation is to tell the world exactly how the people struggle and die in Nicaragua today, and to set our imprisoned comrades free."

The camera swivelled to an ambulance approaching the airplane. The back door was opened and two nurses brought out a stretcher on which lay a youth, a Garand rifle beside him and a red-and-black kerchief covering the lower half of his face.

"The guerrilla who was wounded in the assault on the National Palace has arrived," announced the commentator. "He has come to join his comrades, to travel with them to Panama in the airplane."

---

* Edén Pastora later joined the Contra forces. It was at his press conference at San José in 1984 that a bomb, now believed to have been planted by the CIA, exploded and killed or wounded several of the journalists present.

The camera closed in to focus on the boy's face, as the commentator passed him the microphone.

"Mario!" Armando leapt from his chair. "I swear it's Mario." Armando reached the television in a single bound.

"Do you have anything to say to the viewers of Latin America?" asked the interviewer.

"We will win," replied Mario.

"It *is* his voice," Armando swallowed a sob.

"The plane will land in Panama where President Torrijos has offered asylum to the guerrillas and the political prisoners," the commentator continued.

The image changed and Armando switched off the television.

"We should drink to this," his eyes were wet as he poured the next brandy. "Don't you dare say no, Ximena, I'd never forgive you."

Ximena held out her glass.

"It was Mario, I promise you. I'll prove it to you now."

He put his glass down on the table, bent over to pick up his briefcase, sat down with the album on his knees and began leafing through it with nervous fingers. Ximena leaned over to get a better look.

"Here it is, here it is," Armando put his hand over Mario's mouth and nose, "it was him, I swear, the same look in his eyes, thick eyebrows, the same hairline. It was him, Ximena."

He put the album on Ximena's lap, then raised his glass.

"To the men of the FSLN," his voice was choking, "now on their way to Panama, along with Commander Cero and the others. What luck Mario wasn't seriously injured. Did you notice how steadily he lifted his rifle? Garands are the heaviest."

Ximena turned over another page with a look of surprise.

"Tomorrow I must leave for Panama," Armando's voice was definite, "and you have to help me."

"Why have the faces been cut out of these photos?" asked Ximena.

"Hang on a minute, Ximena. I must see Mario as soon as possible, and talk to Edén Pastora. I can't waste another day."

"Just a minute," Ximena's voice rose. "First tell me why you've cut out all these faces."

Armando exhaled and picked up the album.

"Nothing to do with me. When I first looked at it in Costa Rica I thought Maruca must have done it for security reasons. That would have made sense. All the missing faces belong to comrades in the guerrilla."

"What do you mean "Maruca must have done it?" Aren't you sure now?"

"Not all of them have lost their faces. Only those who've died. Here, for example, is another picture of two comrades with me in Nicaragua," he pointed to a picture of three men around a bar table, "they're Ricardo and Paco, members of the León committee. That's my wife's home town and she's well aware they're working against Somoza. Why didn't she remove their faces, too?"

"What do you mean?"

"I can't really explain it. I just don't think it was her. It just happened, that's all."

Ximena stared at him in disbelief.

"When I began to notice that all the missing faces were of friends who'd either been assassinated or who'd died under torture, I started brooding. Suddenly, one day I was flicking through the album and noticed that Benito's face was missing. Last time it had definitely been there. See here."

He pointed to a photo of himself with a youth whose face had been neatly excised. "After a while I forgot about it until a few months later I got a letter from Maruca saying that Benito had been killed during the assault on the National Guard barracks at Masaya."

Ximena remained quiet.

"You'll think I'm crazy, but to me this photo album is bewitched."

"Armando," Ximena weighed her words carefully, "it's not that I think you're crazy or anything, but you yourself were just telling me of your prison experiences, the torture, memories of dead friends. Such things sometimes seem unbearable. Don't you think it might actually have been you who cut out the faces, to help erase all those memories, and that maybe you then repressed the knowledge of having done it?"

Armando shrugged and shut the album. "Maybe you're right, there must be some explanation, but none of that seems to matter very much right now. I must fly to Panama tomorrow, and I've got barely 250 francs. You must help me out with the ticket."

"What will you do in Panama? If that boy really was Mario, about which I have my doubts, he wasn't seriously wounded. He looked healthy enough to come to Paris and convalesce."

"He'd never do any such thing. As soon as he recovers he'll go straight back in the guerrilla like all the others do."

"And you, what will you do in Panama? You've just told me they don't trust you."

"You don't understand a thing, Ximena. Let me explain. The revolution began last February, after Chamorro's assassination. The FSLN hadn't as yet organized the people into neighborhood committees. There was a spontaneous uprising against Somoza and his National Guard who managed to smash it before the FSLN could step in and offer essential leadership and coordination. I'm sure that error has now been rectified and the operation by Edén Pastora was the signal to trigger the uprising. It's happening, Ximena, don't you see? You'll learn a lot in the next few days, things I won't be able to read about because I'll be with the *guerrilla* and there won't be newspapers. But they need men like me for the next stage. Not just to be an extra rifle, but also because it's essential for them to have a nucleus of committed *guerrilla* with enough experience to raise the morale of the newcomers whenever necessary. That's something the Somozas and the National Guards of this world still refuse to understand. They refuse to because they have no way of fighting it."

"And what's 'it'?"

"They can't deal with the fact that true revolution comes from within, is a solitary and intimate internal revolution that moves us to take a first step that can only be taken in silence, of one's own accord. Something akin to the novice making her first vows. You know the procedure: they cut her hair, recite the prayers for the dead, while she prostrates herself before the altar surrounded by four candles, and they leave her alone there a while to say her prayers and give herself to her mystical spouse. When the others reappear, she's made her vow and is now a bride of Christ. It's the same thing to join the FSLN, only without all the pomp and ceremony. You have to make your commitment and wed death, just like the nun. You know you're laying your life on the altar and from then on your skin won't matter a scrap to you: you've already offered it up for those who will survive to enjoy a better future. That's the step more and more Nicaraguans will be taking in the coming days. Some will take it enthusiastically, others will feel they're doing it from force of circumstance, realizing that Somoza and the National Guard have now declared war on the entire population. They need models, and that's something I may be able to help them with. I've been through it all, Ximena: prison, torture, humiliation and self-doubt. I know how that decision to marry death suddenly sets you free. You leave aside cowardice and fear for your precious skin and you're incorporated into an audacious, invincible organism. Invincible in the sense that every cell of which it's composed has overcome fear and you can direct your energy and concentration on the task at hand: the destruction of Somoza and all he represents."

"But there are always cowards," Ximena objected. "How can you anticipate transforming an entire people in this way?"

Armando shook his head.

"Every war in the history of humanity demonstrates how, once a people loses patience with tyrants, when at long last they wake up to the fact that all they have to lose is fear, and that their lives are incidental, then they take that step and joyfully accept suffering, danger and death in order to achieve

111

victory. Wait and see. Somoza and his clique will prove to be the best trainers and recruiters the FSLN could wish to find. Teachers who, when they take up arms against their own people, sign their own death warrants."

"You're right," replied Ximena. "I admit you've convinced me."

"I hope you also now understand how essential it is for me to leave no later than tomorrow."

"Of course I do. The problem is that I don't have enough in my bank account to pay for your ticket."

"Fair enough," Armando opened his arms wide. "Then Marcel will have to be the victim. After fifteen years' marriage I haven't the slightest doubt that you know exactly how to fleece him for something far less important."

"Let me think," Ximena got up and tiptoed over to Marcel's study, wobbling slightly. Before going into the corridor she turned and looked back at Armando, placing her finger on her lips: "Shh. Absolute silence please."

Marcel wasn't in his study, he'd long since gone to bed. Ximena lit the lamp and opened the desk drawer where he kept his check book. Then she quickly returned to the drawing room and sat down next to Armando on the sofa.

"Damn, the holidays cost us an arm and a leg. Look, here's the balance," she handed the accounts to Armando. "Marcel won't be paid until the end of the month and I don't start earning again until October."

Armando passed back the bank statement and began laughing. "It's all relative. If my bank balance looked like this I'd take you all out to the Tour d'Argent immediately. Sorry, Ximena, I don't want to seem unsympathetic to your problems, but you're my only hope in this damned City of Lights. I know my typewriter isn't worth a lot, but maybe at least you could hock it along with my books. I'll reimburse you as soon as I can."

"Don't worry about it. I don't know how I'll figure it out, but somehow I will."

Armando got to his feet, helped her to hers, and crushed her in his arms. "You're fabulous," he told her, "a true heroine of the resistance. I'll meet you at ten tomorrow outside the Orbis Agency on the Boul. Mich. Agreed?"

"Agreed. I promise. See you tomorrow, Armando."

She switched out the light and went to the bedroom where Marcel lay snoring. She undressed in silence, advanced the alarm clock by 15 minutes and fell into limbo.

Next morning, as the alarm went off, Ximena sat up in bed with a whimper. She felt as though her head was about to explode.

"Armando, Armando," she grunted as she stuffed her feet into her slippers.

"What's up?" asked Marcel, opening his eyes.

"Nothing," she said, dragging herself to the bathroom.

You're a disaster, Ximena, she told herself, looking in the mirror. When will you learn not to mix your drinks?

She took two aspirins with a mouthful of water, dragged a hairbrush through her tangled hair and began to paint on a new face as best she could, in an effort to conceal the evidence of a night's drinking.

While Marcel shaved she went to the kitchen, squeezed two oranges — something unheard-of — and, instead of eating a couple of her daily rusks, carefully cut up the remainder of yesterday's baguette, put it on to toast and prepared the blend of butter, honey and cinnamon that was Marcel's favorite.

"What a treat," he greeted the morning's banquet. "Never was a lord better served by his lady. To what does he owe the honor?"

"To the fact that I love you enormously," she told him with a kiss.

"Did you come to bed very late last night?"

"Yes."

"You should have stayed in bed."

"I'm afraid I've gotten up to extract some money from you," Ximena was shaking.

"Ah, now I understand. That's the reason for so much attention."

"No, honest to God, don't be silly."

"How much do you need?"

"Promise me you won't be shocked."

"First of all remember that ever since the holidays we've been living on thin air."

"What would you have me do? If you insist on having your steak at dinnertime I have to settle accounts with the butcher. He hasn't been paid for nearly two months now, nor the man who delivers our wine. And remember that we still owe on the color television and for your flaming triple-decker record player."

"Mmm," Marcel was stirring his freshly pressed orange juice, "not to mention your everlasting account at the Boutique René. Fine, I don't want to spoil a splendid breakfast. How much do you need?"

"Two thousand five hundred francs," she said, holding her breath.

"What? You're mad."

"I'll show you the accounts tonight," she lied.

Marcel bit savagely into his toast and she ran to his study to find the check book and a pen.

Once Marcel had left, Ximena ran into the bedroom, hurriedly dressed and took the check to the Credit Lyonnais at the corner. There wasn't too much of a line, and it cleared quickly. She put the cash in her bag and went to the nearest taxi stand. Armando had said ten o'clock exactly and he'd be getting impatient.

She found him nervously pacing up and down in front of the travel agency on the Boulevard St. Michel.

"I was beginning to be afraid you wouldn't show up."

"It's only ten-fifteen," she smiled, and gave him a kiss and the 2,500 francs.

"Did you hear the eight o'clock news?" asked Armando, returning the kiss.

"No, I was still sleeping it off."

"I haven't closed my eyes all night long." Armando was pushing his way through the swinging doors. "As soon as I got home I took a couple of aspirins and began getting my stuff together. The news is wonderful, a general strike has started. Do you realize what this means? Bankers, merchants, unions, the lot, committed to our movement. Including the Chamber of Commerce, never in its history known to have lifted a finger against Somoza."

"Good morning," said the clerk, raising her eyes from the desk.

Armando went over to her. "I need to fly out to Panama today. Can I do it?"

"I would think so. We have daily flights to Mexico and from there you can make a connection."

He's sloughing his skin, thought Ximena. All of us are changing. This old world of ours is transforming into something unknown.

"You're in luck," said the clerk, looking at her computer screen. "The Mexico flight leaves at three this afternoon French time, and lands in Mexico at six Mexican time. There's a flight leaving for Panama at eight this very night."

"Perfect. Do I need a visa?"

He can't wait to be off, thought Ximena.

"Yes," replied the girl, "why don't you go to the Consulate now, while I book your flight?"

"What luck," said Armando as they went out to the street. "I'll invite you to a quick coffee here on the corner."

They sat down at a table on the sidewalk and Ximena ordered two coffees with cream while Armando went to the phone booth and began consulting the directory.

What'll I say to Marcel? Yesterday the call to El Salvador and today this. I promised to start saving so we could buy the apartment. He'll never trust me again.

"I'll have to take a taxi to the Consulate." Armando had reappeared and was sitting down next to her. "There are a thousand things for me to do before three o'clock."

"Do you need help?"

"No thanks," Armando was distracted.

He's already gone, she thought.

"I've still got to get home and pick up my suitcase." Armando sighed as he lifted his cup and took a sip.

Locked into his own solitude.

"I'll leave a key with the concierge for you," Armando was still talking to her. "You'll be able to get in for the typewriter, the books and your radio. Do what you think best with them."

"What can I do to be useful, Armando?"

"Don't worry about it," he ruffled her hair, "last night I recruited you. You'll find all the information you need in this briefcase."

"You can count on me."

Armando said nothing.

He's already far away.

"I must be off." Armando was getting up from the table.

"At least drink your coffee." She raised her head to meet his eyes.

"It's getting late." He leaned over and gave her a kiss.

"I'll see you at the airport."

"No, sweet cousin, no. We bade each other farewell last night."

Ximena caught one of his hands in hers and gazed intently at him. "Good luck," she said with wet eyes, "a big kiss to Mario, and write when you can."

"That goes without saying. A hug to Marcel. I hope to repay you soon."

"Don't worry about it." Her eyes followed him out of the café until he disappeared down the street.

Three years in Paris and she hadn't begun to know him until last night.

She hung around a few more minutes in the café, then decided to walk home. The heat was suffocating, but Ximena enjoyed walking through Paris in August. The streets were nearly deserted and one could stroll casually without being infected by the usual bustle.

Better to confront death than to rot away bit by bit, she thought.

By the time she reached the Luxembourg Gardens the briefcase was beginning to weigh her down. She decided to sit down on a wrought-iron chair and watch the children in the paddling pool. They were playing with little boats made of brightly painted wood and paper.

What on earth had he put in the case?

On an impulse she picked it up off the ground, placed it on her knees and opened it. On top of a bundle of papers there was a note that said: "Ximena, with the eyes of the world now on current events in Nicaragua, it's essential that you distribute this information to my journalist colleagues. You'll find their addresses enclosed. The minute I get to Panama, I'll make sure that my comrades there send you the material they want published."

"Vingt centimes," said the chair attendant with a sour look.

Ximena hurriedly returned the papers to the briefcase, hunted through her bag and handed over the money.

"This foul city," she murmured angrily. "They even make you pay for sitting down."

She got up brusquely and set off with determined strides. Armando was right, I should have done the same. Sloughed off my skin, got the hell out of Paris. What am I doing here after all these years?

She walked through the great barred gates and waited for the light to change. The trees were heavy with dark green leaves. The asphalt on the street was shimmering. She visualized Armando on the Panamanian streets, hugging Mario, unable to utter a word.

Students wandered among the open-air cafés dressed in jeans, in great multicolored tunics, in full skirts reaching to their ankles. The light turned green and she hurried to cross the street.

It's the same for all these Africans and Indians. There's nothing for any of us here. I have to free myself from my family, my terrors, my infantile obsessions.

117

The family, that sticky spider's web set to snare us if we don't get out in time.

She paused to look at the window display in a bookshop.

Children crying with hunger are far more important, she told herself, resuming her walk. How come I never managed to have a child?

"Impossible," the doctor had pronounced. "The uterus of a small girl."

Is that what had given her an infantile outlook on life?

Let's just say my maternal instinct was just as undeveloped. Ever since childhood, responsibilities have weighed me down. I dreamt of being Peter Pan. The idea of growing up terrified me, still worse growing old or dying. Ximena, you're self-centered, sinking more and more into your creature comforts. Underneath it all, I love the chains that bind me, they're my excuse for doing nothing. Will Marcel understand this? That it's far more important to breathe fresh air, an air unpolluted by conquistadores or military despots and overseers? That it's much more important not to be gassed by the stench of the rotting room? Amazing how one can change in a single night. Something happens and zip! you turn a somersault in the air and when you land again you're no longer the same person. Life can and must generate electric shocks, it doesn't have to be part of a lethal and senseless routine.

She paused in front of a boutique, and stared unseeingly at the display of suits. Right, she told her reflection in the window, do you dare go through with it?

The reflection smiled and nodded.

Ximena looked up and down the street, retraced her steps and went into the café.

"Can I have a *jeton*, please?" she asked the barman. She went down to the phone booth, put the *jeton* in the slot and dialed the number.

"Hello, Marcel?" Be strong. "I have to confess I deceived you this morning . . . No, dumbo, not with the porter. He's got a double chin. The check you signed wasn't for what I told you. I spent the lot on an air ticket for Armando . . . Aren't you going to say anything? I'll explain it all later. I had to do it. And besides it'll do us good to shed a few inches from our waistlines . . . What? Yes, there is something else. Armando is leaving for Panama in a few hours to rejoin the *guerrilla* and guess who's the new FSLN representative in Paris? I am. Come for lunch and have a bowl of yoghurt and a piece of toast with me and I'll tell you everything . . . Cíao. See you soon."

She replaced the receiver and thought: Right once again, Armando. Leave the fear behind and everything else becomes a lot easier.

She left quickly and nearly ran up the steps to the apartment on the Rue Dauphine.

There was a letter on the floor as she entered. She bent down to pick it up and saw it was from Roberto. At last.

She put the briefcase down on the sofa and opened the letter with nervous fingers. She began reading:

"Dear Ximena, I'm writing to you and Trini to let you in on an event that's bound to make an impression on you. It's to do with Sergio. Recently he's become a shadow of his former self. Three months ago he got a splinter in the index finger of his right hand and since he's a diabetic, it developed into gangrene. The doctor said the whole hand had to be amputated, even a part of his lower arm, and now he's become unbearable.

"All this by way of a preamble to informing you that three days ago he called me to demand that I go and remove Daddy's remains from the Alvarado mausoleum. I asked why and Sergio flew into a rage and told me that the mausoleum was reserved exclusively for the Alvarado family and not for Nicaraguans who turn up penniless in our country to take the bread from our mouths.

"As you can imagine, I also flared up and unleashed a few home truths.

"Today I went and bought a plot in the cemetery and Adolfo is designing a mausoleum for our family. As this'll take a few months to complete, I've decided to remove Daddy's bones as

119

soon as possible to my wife's family mausoleum. I don't want to give crazy Sergio the chance to throw them out in some fit of madness.

"Please don't worry about it. It's all been resolved now, but I wanted you to know the story so you'd realize what kind of human specimen our Uncle Sergio really is . . ."

Ximena put the letter down on the table. The events of the previous night and of this morning had completely wiped out her former obsession. Her fears were without foundation and the entire melodrama, like so many family crises in Santa Ana, had amounted to a tempest in a teapot.

So now it was his right hand. In a few days he'd be serving another banquet to his cronies to celebrate the burial of his arm. Well and good. What could she do? Let the dead bury their dead. Chus was already taking care of them in the other Santa Ana. Here and now she should be helping Armando, trying to do something for that great rotting room of Central America: the great white sepulchre where Uncle Sergios and Somozas are busy robbing the poor of even the air they breathe, accumulating wealth at their expense, until finally they rot away with gangrene.

She sat down at her desk, reopened the briefcase, set aside the letter addressed to her and began leafing through the information bulletins. Naturally enough, they were all dated before the assault on the National Palace.

Only three days since the assault?

Her sense of time had suddenly accelerated and the hours of the last few days had stretched to include more events than she could possibly have anticipated.

Here was something with a very recent date, which had to be of immediate use: the Broad Front's 16-point plan for a peaceful transfer of power from the Somoza dictatorship to a representative democracy. It would be good to translate it into French and circulate it among Armando's journalist friends. It could be useful to them in covering the events of the coming days. She put the bundle of papers aside, and kept that one out.

She'd do it today, after lunch.

She suddenly remembered Armando's face as he said goodbye to her in the street. She pulled the album out from the bottom of the briefcase, put it on the desk and began leafing through it.

There was a photo of Mario in his football uniform. What a handsome young man, she thought. "Good luck," she murmured.

She went back to the beginning of the album, wanting to see the picture of Armando with Maruca and their two children. She discovered a photo of her father she hadn't seen before. There were all the uncles and aunts too, the grandparents and the forty-eight cousins.

She experienced a sense of intense disquiet and pored over the page. It was worse than disquiet, like a sudden somersault inside her.

Slowly she studied the faces in every photo. Her fingers were trembling slightly. What was going on? She continued leafing through.

At last she found what she was looking for. Wide-eyed, she stared at the family group and stopped, immobilized, for several long seconds, as her mind searched for and rejected possible answers.

It was impossible. She exhaled an incredulous sigh and went on and on leafing through. There were the León comrades, their faces intact. There was Maruca, Mario, Hector.

Had he spent the night doing that? No, that was crazy.

She continued slowly turning pages, studying each one methodically with growing incredulity and amazement, until at last she closed it on the final page and sat there staring into space.

Armando's face had been cut out of every single one of the photos.

He won't be long in coming, she could hear Chus' voice.

"How do you say *child* in Nahuatl?" Ximena asked.

Cunet.
"And *cradle?*"
"Tapexco."
"And *guerrilla,* Chus, how do you say guerrilla?"

EPILOGUE

"Somoza travelled with his son, Commander Somoza Portocarrero, and the interim director of the National Guard, his illegitimate half-brother, José Somoza. The airport was full of officers. At approximately 4:30 p.m. an aircraft of the official airline Lanica, a 727, took off with members of the government and civil service and key supporters of the regime. The aircraft also carried two zinc coffins containing the bodies of Anastasio Somoza García and Luís Somoza Debayle, father and brother of the outgoing president."

July 18, 1979

Village of God and the Devil

To Robert and Beryl*

The Barcelós, Marcia jotted down in her notebook about the locals in Mallorca, almost never got to Deyá before June, but this year they had installed themselves by Holy Week. Slim and Marcia only realized this when they came across Tebas, peeing on their books and leaving behind a large pile of shit in the middle of the sheepskin rug.

Tebas was a thoroughbred. He had blue eyes and, according to Slim, was possessed by a soul in torment.

Marcia heard him push the front door open, and raced down from the bedroom just in time to shoo him out with a dishcloth.

Slim and Marcia liked to sleep until nine or ten o'clock, but the Barceló family was of peasant stock and in the habit of rising with the sun. From that moment onwards the Señora would begin shrieking and wouldn't let up for the rest of the day, except during siesta hour.

Last summer, for example, the old man would scarcely have been given his coffee and propped up in the chaise lounge beside the fountain before the old woman started her scolding: "See," she'd shriek, "see how they've neglected the plants." She'd raise her voice even higher than usual so her neighbor Francisca, charged with minding the plants when they spent the winter in Palma, would be sure to hear. "Look at this one," she would hardly lower her voice as she addressed the old man. "All dried out and drooping. Do you know what it reminds me of? Your pathetic little prick that's been shrivelled for years."

And so on in the same vein, every morning.

---

* Robert and Beryl Graves, the English poet and his wife, who lived for over forty years in Mallorca.

However, this year was proving different. Apart from Tebas' morning howls, an unusual silence surrounded Ca'n* Barceló.

Slim and Marcia both commented on it on one of the rare occasions when they had their morning coffee together.

"Perhaps there's been a reconciliation," Slim suggested.

"Nonsense," Marcia replied, "some forces are irreconcilable. It's simply that they're growing decrepit."

This community of ours is an odd lot. Many of its members are approaching their centenary. They are bent, wrinkled, white-haired, but wherever you come across them, climbing up or lumbering down the steep steps up to the town hall, and stop to say "hello" to them, they always reply *"bon día"* and carry on without pausing for breath.

Way up there, on Don Pedro's estates — the church and the cemetery — if we peer through the weeds and the plastic flowers to the lettering on the tombstones we can discover that the youngsters die in their seventies and the majority continue on well into their nineties.

Strange things took place in the village. For example the other day — Marcia hadn't dared mention it to Slim, since he was still engaged in writing the definitive novel about Deyá and she was afraid that if she began he'd keep her there three-quarters of an hour, without letting her go and water her plants, hounding her like a criminal court judge in Palma giving her the third degree. Anyway, what actually happened was quite straightforward. Marcia was climbing up the mule-steps to visit the vegetable lady who happened to be married to the Civil Guard (it was useful to be on good terms with both of them, since he was the one who settled village quarrels); she was climbing up step by step, trying to remember whether Slim wanted parsley or celery-stalks, since he was always so particular over seasoning for the soup. She was pausing every five steps to practise her yoga breathing, her heart pounding slightly at the exercise, but with no sense of hurry because the

* Ca'n: Mallorcan for house.

124

day was fine, the sun resplendent. As she inhaled and counted to four, then slowly emptied her lungs, each leaf of every carob and olive tree all the way to those on the furthest flank of the Teix[*] sparkled with the sun's reflection, and Marcia felt (although she'd never dare say anything of the kind to Slim) she was experiencing what he described as *satori*. She kept on up the stone steps one divided from the next by a mixture of gravel and earth, when suddenly she encountered Don Antonio in his Basque beret, heavily making his way downhill with the help of a cane.

Marcia greeted him with a cheerful "hello" and he returned an absent-minded *"bon día."*

She continued on her way up to the greengrocer's and as she reached the shop she remembered it was a bunch of celery and a clove of garlic that Slim had stipulated for his *pot-au-feu.*

She felt a sense of contentment at having remembered and decided to take a turn around the village on her way down. It was only as she passed René and Huguette's boutique that she remembered suddenly that Don Antonio had been dead these past three months.

He'd fallen gravely ill a few days either before or after Generalissimo Franco had also fallen ill and, between radio bulletins, newspaper headlines and television news reports from the twenty-one doctors in attendance, Francisca went daily to Slim and Marcia's house to report on her father's deterioration and impending death.

Don Antonio had paid dearly for his Republican sympathies during the Civil War. Thanks to the Catalan surname of Castenar, and the ownership of a house and a few terraces of land, he was permitted to remain in the village, but was regarded as a dangerous element. Dangerous despite multiple ailments of lungs, stomach and heart.

---

[*] The Teix is a mountain chain running parallel to the north-west coast of Mallorca.

In his youth he had organized the town band which meant, in those days without electric light, radio, or discotheques, that the eight musicians assembled by Don Antonio had formed the nucleus of the village's social life, the backbone of the fiestas of San Juan and the bonfires of San Sebastian, when loaves 6 feet long were baked and sprinkled with salt and chopped onion, to be consumed around a crackling fire.

The fact remained that Don Antonio outlived the Generalissimo, who'd postponed dying for a whole month, thanks to the assistance of his battery of doctors.

Marcia would go next door to exchange a few sentences now and then with the old man who dozed in his green plastic armchair. His emphysema prevented him from Lying in bed.

"How's the Generalissimo?" he'd always greet her.

Francisca and the rest of his children kept the newspapers from him, to prevent his becoming overexcited.

Marcia would murmur the midday medical bulletin to him and the two of them would exchange conspiratorial looks or shake their heads hypocritically.

Every afternoon at precisely five o'clock the village doctor would arrive and block the road down to the Clot[*] with his car as, daily more reluctantly, he prescribed new injections to perforate Don Antonio's flabby and worn-out flesh.

As the days grew longer and the whole country first waited expectantly and then became bored with the whole business of the monotonous up-and-down bulletins issued from El Pardo, Don Antonio suffered stoically while Francisca bawled at Gabriel, who was just learning to walk.

On the first of the three days of national mourning, Marcia visited Don Antonio to inquire after his health, and he gave her a wink.

"I've won. It's taken me these past forty and some years, but it's an honorable victory. I'll see you tomorrow, God willing."

In the end he had two weeks to mull over his victory and leave behind no possible doubt as to who'd won the final round.

[*] *El Clot*: (literally 'hole') is a sharp drop into the valley below Deyá.

The old grandfather clock in Ca'n Blau, that looked more like a character out of Lewis Carroll than a grandfather clock, had just finished its sonorous tolling of the midnight hour when Francisca arrived to tell Slim and Marcia that it was all over. Her next move was to commandeer the telephone and spread the news to all her numerous friends and relatives scattered around the island.

Marcia dragged Slim away from the fireside where he was huddled with his Sufi readings, to go over to the Castaners.

They went up to the bedroom where Don Antonio was laid out on a sheet on the floor. His son and a son-in-law had put his armchair into the yard and Slim helped them to dismantle the giant double bed.

Francisca's mother, ill and worn-out with having nursed her husband through the preceding seven long weeks, had gone to bed in the adjacent bedroom where her granddaughter slept, and was hardly aware of her husband's death.

Slim emptied the room with the help of Don Antonio's sons. Then, when no piece of furniture remained, they improvised an altar. A neighbor contributed a white embroidered cloth to the arrangement.

When the corpse-dresser arrived, everyone else went down to the kitchen, only Francisca and one of her brothers remaining upstairs. The neighbors began to arrive and Marcia and the fisherman's wife put the coffee on to warm.

An hour later Francisca called downstairs to let them know they could all come up.

Don Antonio had been transformed. He was dressed in a dark grey suit and his features had been subtly altered, giving him the appearance of a gentleman farmer, a man of tranquility and triumph.

The transformation precipitated an outbreak of tears from his daughter-in-law, who suddenly dropped to her knees on the floor and deposited two kisses upon the corpse, one on each cheek.

"Get away from him, what an outrage!" the corpse-dresser squealed, leaping from Gabriel's chair in a single bound, her

127

arms windmilling. "An outrage!" she repeated. "Hasn't anyone ever told you that the dead don't want to be kissed? You must leave the dead in peace once their blood runs cold, so they can free themselves and not be condemned to hang around the house."

Death is taken very seriously here in Deyá. The routine is always the same: empty the room in which the deceased breathed his last; dress him; lay him out on the floor until the coffin arrives from Sóller; improvise an altar and scrupulously scrub the room, to turn it into a kind of austere chapel where the corpse can repose for the night. Meanwhile those attending the vigil come up and pay their last respects, before rapidly descending to drink coffee and brandy with the group at the front door and swap stories of the life and miracles of the deceased.

Not infrequently someone detaches himself discreetly from the group in order to urinate, falls into the streambed, and requires rescuing amid shouts and guffaws.

The following day the coffin is placed in the Land Rover belonging to the municipal secretary, and driven to the church. There a funeral mass is held, followed by the burial in one of the six or seven mausoleums of the families of Deyá. Until a few years ago there was a scandal every time a foreign non-Catholic was careless enough to drop dead in the village. A little plot, barely 9 feet square, surrounded by a thin wall scarcely 2 inches thick and 4 and a half feet tall, protected the Holy Mother Church in all its Catholic, Apostolic and Roman splendor, from the terrible odor of heresy. The plot was soon crowded and they had to start packing them in vertically.

"Just think about it," Slim worried. "It must be awfully uncomfortable, to spend eternity on your feet awaiting the Final Judgment."

The morning after the funeral, the neighbors begin arriving with buckets of lime to whitewash the walls of all the rooms and the corridor along which the deceased has been carried. They open up his mattress, remove the stuffing in order to wash it, and disinfect the furniture in the room where the death has occurred.

One day Marcia asked the village intellectual the whys and wherefores of it all, and he answered that the terror of the Black Death still persisted throughout the island, hence the need to disinfect the houses.

Marcia was surprised. "But no one knew anything about disinfectants during the time of the Black Death."

He began to stammer. "Well, maybe. Perhaps that all came later. In any case, that's the way things are."

When Don Antonio died, Marcia asked Francisca for her explanation of the custom.

"Good grief! Do you think we really need a soul in torment roaming the house? You have to put the dead off the scent so they can find their eternal rest."

According to Robert, the reason for so many strange happenings in Deyá (which means God's Village) was the amount of ferrous oxide in the side of the Teix which loomed above the village. Between the Teix and the sea or, more precisely, in the village itself, this caused a polarization of electromagnetic forces that sharpened the people's sensitivity to an acute degree.

Robert held that this mysterious polarization intensified the natural inclination or inner essence of each of Deyá's inhabitants, whether for good or ill. Naturally enough, plenty of other influences also came into play: the seasons, electric storms, winter humidity, the mistral and sirocco winds, the moon's phases.

Oh come off it! (Marcia was to note at the revision stage of her thesis, some time later.) Dr. Stone always told us that true anthropologists have to abstract themselves from the fundamental equation (taking up a position inside phenomenological parentheses) before getting on with the job. But in the first instance, I have serious doubts as to my capacity ever to comprehend that square-headed German, Husserl, and, worse still, how to abstract myself from an equation like that while I disentangle the extraordinary idiosyncrasies of Deyá, when I realize that if I'd kept my big mouth shut, no one would've rediscovered the philosophers' stone and everything would have gone on as usual.

To be truthful, it's not simply a matter of Deyá itself. The whole northern part of the island is a devil's triangle, just like the Bermuda Triangle, encompassing three villages: Deyá, Sóller and Fornalutx. By way of historical proof of such a triangle, people quote a saying from the sixteenth century that runs: "The Devil takes flight from Sóller, passes over Fornalutx and Deyá to survey his dominions, and returns to Sóller again."

When Slim and Marcia signed the contract to purchase Ca'n Blau, they were already familiar with the Mallorcan habit of celebrating such agreements with a few glassfuls of brandy. They seated themselves on three rickety chairs in the middle of what was going to be their living room, and Slim filled the glasses lent them by their neighbor, Uncle Juan.

Jordi, Can Blau's former owner, raised his glass and remarked that he'd noticed their appreciation of antiques and wanted to bestow on them a pair of extremely ancient doors to ensure the house could be well locked up. "I inherited them from my great-great-grandparents," he vowed. "I reckon they must be at least four hundred years old."

He brought them along in his truck the following day. Marcia duly admired their beauty and over the following days began to polish the old wood, studded with medieval nails, with a mixture of linseed and kerosene.

"The village is going to pot," old Jordi, who now lived in Palma, lamented. "Things have been gradually deteriorating since I was a child. In those days wheat fields were sown on the sides of the Teix and the people climbed to the top carrying their tools, even though it took them four hours to get there. They camped up there during the sowing and harvesting seasons. The women would go up twice a week to take them food. I spent weeks there" — he pointed out a clearing near the summit of the mountain — working at a furnace where charcoal was manufactured. In those days we had to work hard to survive. Now it's a different story. The terraces are abandoned and nobody bothers to rebuild the stone walls when they crumble. Fifteen years ago they were still bringing people from Murcia to pick olives. They used the old crushing mills to extract the oil. Now it's unprofitable and no one even prunes the trees. It's a scandal, the way they're neglected.

"There are olive trees in these parts," he shook his head sadly, "that are more than a thousand years old. The Moors planted them. Although nobody cares for them they still struggle on. They survey us with thousand-year-old patience, knowing full well that they'll still be here long after all of us have gone."

How right our friend is, mused Marcia as she pulled out her comparative anthropology notebook, the number of things those olive trees have witnessed, trees with twisted trunks that once delighted Doré. They were here when the pirates arrived; they were around during the romance between Chopin and George Sand, and perhaps even the hippies offer them some amusement. Every time there's a full moon, any number of stoned hippies strip off their clothes and go howling through the village. The trees must also love Robert dearly. What would they make of the philosophers' stone, of the flying saucers? Robert, in forty years of living in Deyá in a house overlooking the sea, has observed hundreds of flying saucers diving into the sea to reach their submarine base to the north. Slim is certain they don't come from other planets, but are spaceships crewed by time travellers returning to the twentieth century on multiple scientific expeditions to ascertain why we, poor fools, blew our planet to pieces.

How stupid I am. She laid her ballpoint pen aside. Why do I always let my mind wander? At this rate, this blessed thesis will never get written.

She paused a moment in thought and then resumed writing.

All the early settlements of Mallorca (she noted carefully) were built at a reasonable distance from the sea, for fear of pirate raids. Deyá was no exception and suffered raids on numerous occasions.

From the moment the pirates dropped anchor in the Cala and made their way with considerable difficulty up through the Clot to reach the village, there was time enough to lead the women, the old and the children to the *Torre Mora*, and to mobilize the men to defend the village.

Before the days of mortars and gunship helicopters, the Moorish Tower was an impregnable bastion. It emerges from a hill behind Es Moli: a vertical needle of pure rock some 15 feet in height. At its summit there is a rectangular walled platform that can afford cover to some sixty or seventy people.

Its sole point of access is a flight of narrow steps hewn into the rock face. To reach the platform one has to haul oneself up with both arms and then push upwards. Naturally enough, it was not a feat I could manage. A single man armed with a sabre could defend the fortress against all comers.

The circular towers that adorn the island are lovely. They were constructed in the middle of the sixteenth century, when the Turkish and Berber fleets were marauding in the Mediterranean. Each tower was in sight of the next and they were manned night and day throughout this unsettled period of history. The signalling system was highly efficient. By day they used smoke signals and by night bonfires. Palma's military garrison could be alerted within 20 minutes from any point along the coast.

Sóller, 7 miles northeast of Deyá, boasted the only cove along the length of the north coast in which ocean-going ships could seek haven. Sóller's legendary hero was a one-legged drunk who'd once been a naval cannoneer. At a crucial moment in the village's history he alone knew how to load, aim and fire the old bronze cannon situated on a point overlooking the mouth of the channel. One midday the village elders paid him an urgent visit with the information that a pirate ship was heading towards Sóller and they had need of his services.

The old man, aware of his strong bargaining position, agreed on condition that he was carried to the point on a stretcher and provided with a bottle of *Anís del Mono*. The elders accepted at once and the old man, bolstered with cushions, took nips from the bottle all the way.

By the time he had supervised the initial operations the pirate ship had entered the channel and was preparing to drop anchor. He casually sighted the cannon, ordered his helpers to elevate it a bit, lit the fuse, and the cannonball blew the ship's mast in two. The pirates frantically cut away the tangled sails, weighed anchor, took out their oars and beat an ignominious retreat, never to return again.

As Marcia weeded the plants on her balcony she noticed an eagle wheeling in slow circles over the Teix. She suddenly remembered she'd been neglecting her tree and decided to pay it a visit that same morning. Gardening fork in hand, she tiptoed upstairs to the study and removed the binoculars from Slim's closet.

"After the birds again?" he inquired, looking up.

"Mm. Have you seen the eagle?"

"You're right, there he is," he looked out of the window, "I haven't seen him in months."

"He probably got bored with the view from the Foradada," and she leaned over to kiss his incipient bald spot. "Work hard, I'll be back in time for lunch."

She paused in the bathroom to rinse out an empty bottle of *Je Reviens*, then went down to the kitchen where she filled it carefully with brandy. She screwed the top on tightly and stowed it with the binoculars and the fork in her basket. She paused again to rummage through and make sure she had her cigarettes and lighter, then swung it on to her shoulder.

Not even Slim was party to her secret.

As usual she stopped briefly behind Ca'n Oliver and took a moment's rest to make absolutely sure no one was watching. Then she took the path through the weeds to the terraces that surrounded the hill on the other side of the village. The climb was beginning to make her breathless. An interminable flight of little stone steps led from one terrace to the next. At the top she sank down gratefully, leaned back against the tree trunk and inhaled the pine-scented air.

From here the village seemed a haphazard agglomeration of dolls' houses leading downhill through the Clot and arranged in somewhat more orderly file along the terraces that ran around the peak of the Puig. The narrow ribbon of asphalted road wandered through the valley, reappearing at Ca'n Quet, climbing to Es Moli and curving close by the mountain stream, before streaking back between the shops and disappearing in the direction of Sóller.

From her vantage point under the giant tree Marcia was invisible to the people below, unless she dressed in white, something she was careful never to do on these expeditions.

Thanks to her binoculars she could watch the activities of people in every corner of the village. For example, at this very moment Laura of las Palmeras was gesticulating and doubtless bawling in *mallorquín* at Señora Marroig across the road while Mad Miguel, having finished his café-cognac, was slowly weaving his way down the Clot towards his house. And there was Snow White on her motorbike. She passed Miguel's house and stopped in front of Ca'n Blau. There'd be letters awaiting Marcia's return.

The tree's rough bark comforted Marcia, as did its shade, the whisper of the breeze in its fragrant branches and the cushion of fallen needles on which she was sitting. She was used to going there once or twice a month, whenever she was enmeshed in a problem or felt a burning need to drop her social mask and merge again with the sharp greens, browns and greys of the landscape. She turned to gaze through the branches at the summit of the Teix. The eagle, having accomplished his mission, had disappeared. Now it was her turn.

She took the gardening fork out of her basket, got up and circled the base of the tree, stopping to pull up the weeds that had grown there since her last visit. She worked her way methodically around its perimeter, clearing a wide circle around the trunk. Actually, the ground was very stony and there was a minimal risk that a fire could reach the base of the tree, but Marcia was troubled by the encroaching weeds.

Having finished, she straightened, stretched slowly and went back to her basket. She replaced the fork and took out her flask. She found the exact spot between two protruding roots and poured a stream of brandy onto the earth.

No doubt some would call me crazy, she thought, but for me this is a gesture of friendship and deference to my old and respected neighbor, Sea Eagle.

She returned to her place beside the trunk, put the empty flask back in her basket and sat down again, her back bolt upright and her legs crossed in lotus position. She closed her eyes, breathed rhythmically and, within moments, became aware of the presence of Sea Eagle. He was squatting, aboriginal fashion, his feet planted on the ground, arms wrapped around his knees, as he looked gravely out to sea.

It wasn't that Marcia really *saw* him. That had only happened once in her dreams, but now she was fully conscious of his presence, down to his exact position.

Good morning, Sea Eagle, she greeted him silently.

Bon día, Marcia. His greeting was also silent. Sea Eagle is pleased to acknowledge your libation.

It is given with great pleasure.

Sea Eagle rocked himself back and forth, supporting himself on his heels. I called you because I know you are worried.

"It's Robert," Marcia burst out. "He's getting old and ill. What's going to become of us when he dies?"

Sea Eagle scrutinized the long line of the horizon.

"Someone else will come. That's how it works."

"But who? I can't think of anyone with his strength and wisdom. Stephen's sweet but — how shall I put it? — too obsessive in certain ways."

"It won't be Stephen," Sea Eagle emphasized.

"Everyone's getting nervous. During winter life's easy here, but from June onwards everything changes as hordes of tourists start arriving from England, France and Germany, and there's not a café left one can get into. Every year you hear more German spoken. The tourists are ruining the place and they couldn't care less."

"Be patient," advised Sea Eagle.

"The village still hasn't claimed its blood victim for the year and we're all afraid."

"Don't get upset over nothing," murmured Sea Eagle, blending with the whisper of the breeze among the branches as he disappeared, leaving Marcia alone below the huge tree.

She muttered disconsolately and opened her eyes. It was always reassuring to chat with the old man, yet for once he'd offered no useful advice. She stretched her legs, took a cigarette from the packet and lit it. No matter, in any case Sea Eagle was the perfect tree guardian. She'd often looked up from her terrace at Ca'n Blau and worried about the little groups of people strolling through the terraces out to the promontory, but nobody ever reached her tree: either the weeds and brambles prevented them — or Sea Eagle offered them another more enticing objective.

In a sudden fit of enthusiasm, Slim had planted a vast quantity of vegetables on the terrace they had bought behind Ca'n Blau. That first summer they showered their neighbors with tomatoes, lettuces, carrots, onions and radishes, until the vegetable lady chided them, in the nicest possible manner, that they were undermining her business. Ever since then Slim had planted only enough for their own needs, leaving Marcia space for the flowers she loved so much.

It wasn't an economically viable proposition. Both he and Marcia put in many hours of work in return for the meagre kilos of fruit and vegetables they might have bought for a few hundred pesetas, but Slim insisted proudly on the need to maintain the kitchen garden and Marcia followed the doctor's advice and catered to her husband's whims.

Slim had also wanted to have a hen house and to breed rabbits, but here Marcia drew the line.

"We need protein sources for after the Apocalypse," he protested. "With chickens and rabbits we'd be able to create a closed ecological circle. They'd provide the fertilizer I need to keep the plants growing."

"No chance," Marcia replied. "Neither you nor I are capable of killing and skinning a rabbit we've raised ourselves, nor of wringing the neck of a chicken that has laid our breakfast eggs and plucking it. If it's protein you're after, you'll have to be content with sowing beans."

The reason Slim and Marcia had bought Ca'n Blau and its adjoining terrace, the reason why they'd come all the way to Mallorca and set up home in Deyá in the first place, was Slim's mystical experience some ten years earlier.

Marcia recalled that whole tormented period with distaste. It happened while they were living in Paris. As Slim was voyaging through the fifth dimension, touring in his astral body, he had come to realize that the planet was condemned and the Apocalypse was approaching. With considerable hesitation, he described his experiences to Marcia. He'd since forgotten it all as a result of the electric shocks that had restored him to sanity.

While his physical body lay in a catatonic state in the hospital bed and the nurses fed him through a nose tube, he experienced a vast cosmic vision of the universe, from his vantage point in the *Eternal Now*. He could clearly observe all the ills of the planet and the inevitability of the impending Apocalypse.

"From my privileged position," stammered Slim while recuperating, "it was as though the whole earth were a giant septic tank in which noxious gases were boiling and bubbling as minuscule humans scrambled desperately to save themselves, clutching at rafts of excrement or scrambling through islands of evil-smelling muck."

It was only when Marcia realized that leaving Slim in the hospital another month would plunge them both into bankruptcy that she unwillingly accepted Dr. Buxton's prescription for Slim's recovery.

The prescription — a miraculous one according to the doctor — consisted of a series of massive electric shocks to the brain.

During the first two days of the treatment Slim didn't react. Once the galvanic contortions and horrific grimaces that accompanied them were over, the patient simply resumed a fetal position, regressing to the ineffable zone where cosmic reality was revealing itself to him.

It was the third shock treatment that finally restored him to consciousness. He had barely awakened before he began insulting the doctor.

"Why don't you leave me alone? Can't you see I've no intention of returning to this damned world?"

The doctor, naturally enough, only shot him an ironic glance before continuing with the treatment.

Slim finally decided that cooperation was the best policy. He had no desire to let them fry what remained of his brains. Yet in each of his daily psychotherapy sessions he bitterly bemoaned the world to which he'd been forcibly returned.

Doctor Buxton put up with a week of Slim's incoherent babbling, while growing increasingly worried. Finally he decided to call Marcia in and speak to the two of them together.

"I've analyzed the case," he informed them laconically, "and I'm afraid I haven't gone deep enough. We'll have to excise his remaining memories, otherwise he'll never know peace and tranquility. And there's something else," he frowned, turning to Slim. "You have an overdeveloped critical faculty that will continue to cause you trouble. I want to get rid of that along with all the rest. You'll have to sign this authorization."

He held out the form to them and a week later pronounced Slim fully cured. Apart from having lost all memory of his mystical experiences, as well as a large proportion of his earthly ones, Dr. Buxton was right: Slim was far better adapted to the world. He barely felt a beatific warmth in the cardiac region when he tried in vain to remember the details of his journey through the inner universe, and the loss of his critical faculties didn't worry him in the least.

He was no longer certain how Judgment Day would come about. The most logical cause would be a thermonuclear war; another possibility was that the increasing mass of Antarctic ice would destabilize the planet's rotation and provoke a sudden toppling of the earth's axis.

Be that as it may, Slim was determined to flee from Paris with Marcia, and find a place where they could be safe from the destruction wrought by the impending planetary cataclysm. The doctor had already warned Marcia that Slim's convalescence and recuperation depended on her to a great extent and that she should humor his whims, however eccentric and absurd they might seem.

So Marcia, who had always enjoyed living in Paris, began to pack up all the books and records in their apartment, while Slim spent his days in the Bibliotheque Nationale, submerged in books on cosmology and geography.

"The hour of choice has arrived," he announced one night as he pored over an atlas spread on the table. "If it's a nuclear war, the best place to sit it out would be on an island free of military bases and with minimal strategic importance. It should be situated in a temperate zone and be large enough to provide a sufficient supply of agricultural products. The probable effect of polar change is a different and far more complicated matter. The last time it occurred," here he turned the pages until he came to a map of Africa, "the North Pole was here, somewhere around Lake Chad. That was the catastrophe that culminated in Atlantis, but thousands of years later, in the time of Plato, there was still enough fresh water from the ice meltdown for the whole country around the lake to be fertile. Hippopotamuses, elephants and giraffes inhabited the lakeside in a region that's now one of the most inhospitable and barren on the planet."

Slim coughed and assumed his professorial expression, something he always did when presenting a particularly dubious thesis.

"The problem consists in the following: when, in the blink of an eye, the poles have toppled to create a new Equator, the meltdown will raise the water level of the world's oceans by approximately sixty feet. One can also reckon on earthquakes, tidal waves and cyclonic storms as the planet tilts violently and seeks its new axis. Given all this, we'll need to look for a spot at least a hundred feet above sea level, and accumulate a stock of food sufficient to meet our needs for a year, just like the Mormons do."

Slim showed Marcia his calculations, convincing her that the new North Pole would be situated more or less where Los Angeles is now, and that the isle of Mallorca would find itself some 15 degrees above the new Equator, with a new subtropical climate and considerably greater humidity than at present.

That was how they came to live in Mallorca. Within less than two months from their arrival, Ca'n Blau had been bought and Slim was overseeing its reconstruction.

When Slim and Marcia first got to know the Barceló family, Slim was finishing the redesign of Ca'n Blau and had two options for installing the water supply.

"You can get it from Old Tobias," Pepe Fernandez informed him, "but watch out! That old fellow has already sold more water than there is in his spring and from August onwards all the families in the Puig begin to feel the scarcity. If you get yourself connected to Ca'n Barceló, you'll have a steady flow and won't run short of water in summer."

He gave them the address in Palma, and the copy of a draft contract.

A few afternoons later Slim and Marcia went down to meet the Barcelós. The Señora wore the pants in the family, while Señor remained huddled in an armchair. After Slim and Marcia had agreed to their price and signed the contract, the Señora suddenly acknowledged her husband's presence and, as though apologizing for her absent-mindedness, said: "He has to take good care of himself, poor thing. He has a bad heart."

The figure in the armchair stirred unexpectedly. "Yes," he announced in a thick voice. "Three years ago I suffered a heart attack and when I came out of the clinic I discovered they had installed a little machine in here" — he tapped his chest delicately — "it's a sort of electric clock that controls my heartbeat. Come here," he addressed Marcia, "come over and touch it."

Marcia obeyed with a mixture of timidity and disgust. She placed her hand on the man's chest as lightly as she could, but he caught it in one of his, pulling it down to where his paunch began (the point at which the machine had been implanted) and forced Marcia's fingers to burrow into his flesh so she could give it a good feel.

Señora Barceló observed them with a strange light in her eyes, and the two of them began to laugh. They called Slim over so that he could try it as well, relishing their surprise.

"I'm so happy you bought Ca'n Blau," Señor Barceló told them. "Even though you're young, I can tell that you're sensible types and nothing like the hippies around here."

If he only knew of my days as a flower child in Haight-Ashbury, Marcia thought as she suppressed a smile, or about Slim's cosmic illumination while we were living in Paris.

Robert is convinced I'm a hamadryad (Marcia noted in her private journal), and it seems the most natural thing in the world to him.

"There are plenty of hamadryads at large in the world," he had told her as they strolled downhill through the Clot, talking above the noise of the stream. "It's a shame that so few of you are able to realize your true nature. When you have found your tree," he peered at her from beneath his Cordoba hat, "you must be extremely careful not to reveal your secret to anyone, not even Slim. If anyone finds out which tree corresponds to which hamadryad, that person is endowed with a power of life and death over you."

Marcia was petrified. She took time finding her tree, but once found she had not the least doubt it was the right one. It taught her a lot about the vegetable world, things she'd never previously suspected. Any time she transplanted, watered or dusted the leaves of her plants, she was aware that her tree knew what she was doing.

A tree's roots function as a sensory system (Marcia resumed writing). Thousands upon thousands of interconnected roots weaving nets of vegetational ganglia to form a vast unbroken carpet. Forest trees learn to understand sheep better than humans. The smaller animals live in close symbiosis with the vegetable world. They remove grass and weeds to give room for new growth and clear a vital living space beneath each tree. Cultivated trees, particularly fruit trees, retain a closeknit friendship with the humans who turn over the soil which leaves their roots free to breathe. They feel grateful to people who provide them with fertilizer and water, who pick the fruit that begin to weigh them down, who prune their dry branches.

Whoever takes care of trees in the countryside is adopted by one of them and from that time onwards that tree is inhabited. Uninhabited trees are never able to comprehend the extraordinary gift of locomotion. Contemplation of animal activity amuses them, even excites their admiration, but it is not something they actually comprehend. For them the animal kingdom is the fifth dimension. Their own continuum is rooted and motionless, except for the occasional shaking produced by the wind. The only way in which a tree ascends from one plane to the other is when it adopts a human being and carefully records that person's memories in the rings that form every year in its trunk.

From the day when her tree adopted her, Marcia realized that the old myth of the hamadryads was a distortion of the truth. It wasn't true that if a tree died, so did its human alter ego. What happened was that when an adopted human died his spirit, meaning the essence of the personality, remained cloistered in the tree and from there motionlessly watched over his children and descendants, sharing their sufferings and joys.

142

Take Uncle Juan, for example. He never had any children. He lived his whole life with his deaf-and-dumb sister and perhaps this — the enforced silence in the house — was the reason why he was such a chatterbox when he went out. He had an extraordinary memory. He could remember the whole panorama of events that had passed before his eyes, together with their precise dates. He could also remember every popular legend, and on summer evenings, before it was time for dinner, the children would badger him for stories.

Slim always laughed at the tale of Tomeu Castaner, the friendly giant who, before Marcia's astonished eyes, single-handedly lifted up the rear end of a badly parked truck blocking the way down into the Clot, shifting it out of the way so that his truck could get through. He was as sentimental as he was strong: at times to the point of weakness. The tiniest cut or scrape sent him scurrying to his mother, whimpering pathetically. Uncle Juan told of how one night, as he was playing cards in the bar, Tomeu had been assailed by a drunken tourist looking for trouble. Tomeu got up, asking the tourist if he'd kindly stop bothering him, and his adversary started throwing punches in all directions. Eventually Tomeu lost patience and, advancing as inexorably as a tank or steamroller, told the man: "Kindly do me the favour of leaving." He kept advancing, bumping the foreigner with his stomach: "Please, not in here." Another bump: "We're causing a nuisance." Another three or four bumps and he had him on the terrace where he corralled him up against a stone wall. There he towered over the tourist, taking considerable care not to lay a finger on him, and leaned forward to expel all the air from the man's lungs, leaving him horizontal and gasping on the flagstones.

Slim and Marcia came to know Uncle Juan shortly before he died. It was when Marcia discovered her tree that she renewed her friendship with the old man. Their two trees were neighbors and Uncle Juan, a chatterbox to the last, told Marcia's tree stories that alternately made her laugh and misted her eyes with tears.

How I'd love to share all this with Slim, she thought to herself, setting down her pen. But no, I must be strong. Even at the best of times, Slim is very headstrong and I don't dare subject myself to his whims.

Two days earlier, Slim and Marcia had gone up to Stephen's house for tea. Stephen always laid the table for eight or ten, but as a rule no one turned up, apart from Robert and the occasional Messiah passing through Deyá. Except for Jim, who spent his life wandering about seeking signs to confirm his thesis that the end of the world was at hand.

Robert appeared daily, consumed at least three slices of toast spread with a mixture of butter and honey (the speciality of the house), and slowly sipped his tea. Without a doubt, Stephen was the expert where tea-making was concerned.

Slim and Marcia were his only visitors that afternoon. Robert was away in Palma, a trip that he detested having to make. From the moment Stephen opened the door, Marcia could tell he was overjoyed at having someone to talk to, but he restrained himself until the tea was made and the baguette of wheat bread sliced into thick circles.

Stephen sat facing them across the long wooden table that he'd built himself (he was also an amateur carpenter and antique furniture restorer), and asked them — wide-eyed — if they'd heard the latest news.

"You mean the latest sterling crisis?" Slim asked. Despite having undergone his enlightenment and despite all his Sufi texts, he kept close track of the stock market.

"No," sniffed Stephen, who barely had two coins to rub together and who watched his income evaporate ever more swiftly each month. "I mean what happened on the Puig."

"What happened?" Marcia was interested.

"The poltergeist from number four has moved into number three and is making mischief. Sally and Vicky were there with their friends last night, when suddenly one of them had to go to the bathroom. You both know what a bother that is, the bathroom being all the way outside. Going downstairs, Sally was surprised to find a chair lying across the bottom of the staircase, but she picked it up and went outside without thinking anything of it. When she got back, she discovered that someone had locked the door from the inside. She started shouting for someone to come and open up, but no one heard her because they were listening to records."

"And no doubt they were all stoned," added Slim.

"Eventually, when the music had finished, one of them came downstairs," Stephen continued. "They turned on the lights and found the entire contents of the old sea chest scattered over the floor. And the poltergeist, as usual, had disconnected the bucket from its chain and dropped it into the cistern."

"Are you sure she wasn't just freaked out?" asked Slim.

"I'm sure," Stephen shot him an impatient look. "When Sally tripped out a couple of months ago, she swore she'd never take LSD again. The problem is in the cistern." Stephen was growing still more intense. "Do you remember Ruth? She lived there for months and used to consult the ouija board. That told her the problem was in the water tank."

"You see, Slim?" Marcia interrupted. "This really is the village of God and the Devil."

"Of who?" Stephen's interest was aroused.

"Of the Devil. Carlos Obregon, the fourth Messiah to appear in Deyá, committed suicide by plunging headlong into that very water tank."

"Yes," added Stephen, "but what you don't know is that the tank runs below both houses, and I'm certain that when Don Pedro and Robert conducted the exorcism ceremony in number four . . ."

"What?" Slim was startled. "Robert took part in an exorcism ceremony with Don Pedro?"

"Of course," Stephen's eyes widened as he looked intently at them. "Don Pedro is a little short on both wits and Latin. After Ruth miscarried, what with all the mischief caused by the poltergeist, Robert invited her to his house to recover and Don Pedro went around to her place to conduct the exorcism."

"Ruth was one of his Muses, wasn't she?" Marcia was curious.

"How do I know?" said Stephen impatiently. "But since then no more mischief has been recorded at number four. Presumably the tormented soul retired to the end of the tank underneath number three."

"Meiwa's house," Marcia was taken aback. "Do you remember when she lived there she'd complain that at ungodly hours of the night a ghostly hand would strike chords on the piano and that she was always discovering obscene drawings on the walls?"

"Yes," Slim replied, "but when her husband Larry came home and blocked up a hole in the back patio that was large enough for a child to squeeze through, all the ghostly apparitions stopped."

"Larry has an extremely strong personality, perhaps that was the decisive factor," mused Stephen.

At that instant there was a knock at the door. Marcia was certain that it would be Robert and rose, overjoyed, to let him in. She had just finished reading *The White Goddess* and had a thousand questions to ask him.

When the rebuilding work began in Ca'n Blau, Slim and Marcia rented an apartment in Ca'n Fusimanyi to be close at hand.

Ca'n Fusimanyi was a lovely stone country house dating from the sixteenth century that belonged to the Visconti family, who now had few descendants left in Deyá. Over the doorway hung their coat of arms, bearing the motto "By force or by guile," from which the name "Fusimanyi" derived.

According to the Mallorcans, Cagliostro lived there while he was searching for the manuscripts of Raimundo Lulio to further his alchemical researches. They claimed that Picasso also lived there incognito, not to mention Salvador Dali and Don Santiago Rusinol.

The house now belonged to a priest living in Palma, whose mother was charged with taking care of it and meticulously selecting the tenants. According to her the house was stuffed with treasures and it was not a matter of letting just anybody come and live there.

During their European vacation, Janice and John, friends from California, would pass through Mallorca. Marcia invited them to spend a few days with her. Janice was her closest friend. They'd been San Francisco flower children together, and attended Dr. Stone's classes together, for whom Janice was now an assistant.

They had scarcely put down their suitcases before Janice began a detailed examination of the ornaments and pictures in the sitting room. The walls were covered with seascapes and prints of saints. The shelves were full of Mallorcan plates, some of which were genuine antiques.

All of a sudden a small square mirror hanging on a side wall aroused Janice's interest. She collected mirrors and was delighted with her find. It was an eerie sort of a mirror, one of those fogged ones that can eventually hypnotize a person. Marcia had taken a dislike to it at first sight and even felt a kind of repugnance towards it. She had thought of removing it from the wall during their stay. Janice, in contrast, spent a lot of time simply gazing into it and swearing that she saw hallucinatory images. One day, before boarding the plane for California, she announced to everyone that she couldn't live without the mirror and had decided to take it with her. After all, it was nothing of any intrinsic value.

Slim, John and Marcia all tried to dissuade her, but she took no notice. As she was pregnant, they were loath to argue with her. Janice offered to pay for the mirror, but Marcia knew perfectly well that the priest and his mother had no intention of selling it. Payment would only complicate matters even more. After all, probably no one would even notice. Janice stashed it carefully among her clothes and closed the suitcase. That night the four of them went out to eat at Ca'n Quet. Some time after half-past twelve, when Janice went up to bed, she found an armless rag doll under her pillow. She let out a scream of horror and threw it out the window. John attempted to comfort her, telling her that no doubt some little girl had forgotten it there. But Janice insisted that it hadn't been there when they arrived, and that she'd made the bed every day and never come across it before.

Slim was disturbed by the incident. When they were alone, he informed Marcia that Cagliostro had used mirrors and water vessels for the purpose of clairvoyance and it was well known that dolls were particularly dangerous objects. However, the two of them decided that they oughtn't to add to Janice's already heightened nervous tension and they went to sleep.

Five months later, in a San Francisco hospital, Janice gave birth to a little girl without arms.

Long before Slim and Marcia arrived in Deyá (Marcia noted in her book of local legends), before direct telephone lines had been installed, an event occurred that shook every inhabitant of the accursed triangle.

The telephone operators in Deyá, Fornalutx and Sóller were real witches and listened in on every conversation, however trivial. Their houses were meeting places for old women in search of gossip.

The Fornalutx operator had a daughter who fell madly in love with a Civil Guard who was stationed there to keep public order. The poor girl did everything she could to attract his attention, but he never took the least notice of her. The Guard, a slender youth with true Murcian charm, was in love with the dark and lanky daughter of the Justice of the Peace. Nobody knew exactly what happened, but what is certain is that the operator's daughter, feeling scorned, shut herself up in her room and refused to emerge. A week later, during the full moon, the Justice of the Peace's daughter overturned a table covered with glasses and bottles on the terrace at the Café Deportivo, and ran out into the street howling like a she-wolf, tearing off her clothes. She ran stark naked in the direction of the cemetery. The good ladies sitting in their observatory chairs along the pavement finally managed to stop her in her tracks, wrap her in a blanket and return her to her parents, who, stricken and tearful, locked her up in her bedroom.

Before seven o'clock mass the following morning, the priest came across the young Civil Guardsman embracing a headstone in the cemetery. He was weeping bitterly and his blue-black hair had miraculously turned white.

"Look who's coming," Slim nudged Marcia.

It was a fine June morning. The sea was calm, an intense blue, and there was almost no one on the beach.

Marcia looked again. Deyá's St. John the Baptist, with coppery hair reaching to his shoulders and a long pale-blue tunic, passed by them unseeingly. He was barefoot and appeared to be gliding across the rocks. He paused to chat for a few minutes to Stephen, who was looking for seashells and pebbles at the water's edge. (Stephen had the finest collection of sea-washed stones in all Deyá.) He continued walking in the water up to his ankles before stopping again in front of Patrick and Jamie, two little demons dedicated to rendering life impossible for everyone else. He laid his hands on each of their heads and then disappeared behind the rock that Robert used as a diving platform.

Patrick and Jamie stopped their mischief-making as though enchanted and stared after him, stupefied.

"He's going to pull off a miracle," said Slim. "Just watch and in a minute he'll appear walking on the water."

Marcia burst out laughing and greeted June Redgrave, who was settling herself on an adjacent rock. June was a celebrated actress. She'd lived in Deyá for many years, alone in a house well away from the village, her only companions being a canary and a gigantic one-eyed turkey that strutted airily about the garden.

Every evening, at about seven o'clock, June put on an evening dress and, if it was winter, lit the fire, prepared two Bloody Marys and sat down to chat with her favorite friends: sometimes Errol Flynn, sometimes Cary Grant. Her most constant companion was Victor Mature, with whom June

149

spent many unforgettable hours reminiscing over the Hollywood of their heyday.

"No sign of St. John," said Marcia nervously after a pause, "could he have drowned?"

Slim shivered. Deyá had not yet selected its annual victim.

"Why don't we go and look for him?" Marcia suggested. At that moment the head of St. John the Baptist appeared. He was frog-stroking and his sky-blue tunic floated behind him on the water.

Miramar was a fascinating old house (Marcia noted in her exercise book). The Blessed Raimundo Lulio, in addition to being an illuminati and a Sufi, was the alchemist who fabricated the philosophers' stone. Lulio had built Miramar in 1237 to be the first institute of oriental languages in Europe. Later it served as a monastery for a long time. Its lovely archaic chapel is still in existence, along with a file of Gothic columns and arches that ran alongside what was once the cloister.

Ben Austin and his wife Ruth (who turned out a pornographic novel every three months for their California publisher) moved in there. Two weeks later, in the midst of a terrible electric storm, a ray of lightning split one of their bedroom walls.

"What am I getting into?" Marcia wondered aloud. "This should have been written down in my notes on the resident foreigners. Well never mind. I'll sort it out later."

At that time (she went on writing), the orgies and Black Masses that were to become the fad of certain sophisticated circles in Deyá had not yet begun.

Ben Austin never broadcast the weekly activities taking place in Miramar, but neither did he take pains to conceal them. He invited along any attractive hippy female who turned up in the village, with or without her boyfriend, to witness the formidable prowess of Tony de las Cabras, to whom Ben had awarded the starring role.

The orgies went on throughout the autumn and winter, but over the New Year Ben and Ruth decided to separate. Ruth was becoming bored with the constant weekend parties, and Ben was becoming irrationally jealous of Tony.

When Ruth moved into the poltergeist house in the Puig, Angela moved into Miramar and the orgies took on a still more frenetic pace.

She and Ben planned a special *mise en scène* for Good Friday. According to the widespread rumors circulating afterwards, they were intending to celebrate a Black Mass using the dining table as an altar. They covered it with a white tablecloth stained with menstrual blood. On it a magnificent banquet was to be spread to tempt those who weren't either too drunk or drugged to have entirely lost their appetites.

On Good Friday morning Ben and Angela drove into Palma to buy the last of the delicacies. Ben was stoned as usual and was maneuvering crazily along the edge of the vertical drop.

Slim and Marcia scarcely knew him. They'd seen him once, when he turned up drunk at a poetry reading at the house of some friends. He'd started making fun of everyone, frequently interrupting the reading with ironic compliments. He seemed like one of those would-be-shocking children who only feel really alive when they're kicking or punching a human adversary or tearing apart some piece of conventional wisdom. Slim detested this form of behavior. Ever since his enlightenment he'd avoided such people.

Angela later admitted how terrified she'd been by Ben's driving that day. It amused him to scare her and she knew that showing her fear only made him worse.

"What do you think?" asked Ben, as they caught up with a slow truck straining towards the blind curve at the approach to the municipal reservoir. "Shall we show this moron what we're made of?"

"If you like," Angela replied resignedly.

Ben accelerated, cut to the left to pass and drove his car straight beneath the enormous wheels of a bus full of tourists.

He was decapitated and died instantly. Angela was less fortunate. She remained in a coma for the next four weeks, suffered from hallucinations for two drawn-out months and ended up spending a total of six months in the hospital, with both legs broken and her pelvis so badly shattered it would never fully heal.

Francisca declared that it was divine punishment, that the fiesta they were to celebrate should never have been allowed to take place on a Good Friday.

A few weeks after the Barcelós had returned to Deyá for the summer, Marcia went down to the kitchen for a second cup of coffee (on which she was utterly dependent while she was writing her thesis), and commented to Francisca, who was there washing dishes, about the unusual calm then reigning at Ca'n Barceló.

"Yes," Francisca concurred, "everyone's treating the old fellow with great kindness, so that his last days may be pleasant."

"His last days?" Marcia was surprised. "I knew he'd had a brain hemorrhage, but I thought he was getting over it."

"That's all okay, but now he has a problem with his cardiac battery. When he was in the hospital the doctor warned the Señora that his left side would be paralyzed for the rest of his life and, since their apartment in Palma is on the third floor and there's no lift, she decided that it would be best to simply let the battery run down."

"How horrible!"

"When the old fellow asked his wife if it wasn't time to change it, she replied that the doctors had already done it while he was unconscious in the hospital." Francisca laughed. "Since he has no sense of feeling on his left side, he thought it must be true, but now his eighteen months have nearly run out."

Señor Barceló was fortunate in that his battery lasted nearly nineteen months, the last two of which were tranquil, filled with love and demonstrations of affection on the part of his neighbors. When at last the machine stopped, Slim and Marcia went to the wake and the Señora was inconsolable: shouting, crying and nearly fainting into the arms of the female neighbors striving to calm her.

Slim seemed worried when they returned to Ca'n Blau. Marcia asked him what was wrong.

"It's not uncommon for a worn-out battery to recharge itself on its own, but it would have been cruel to frighten the poor widow with that possibility," he replied.

Elliot Thompson accompanied Bill Waldren's gnomes to the archaeological excavation in the enormous cave underneath Son Rullan. It was a cemetery dating from the Stone Age. As usual, Elliot refused to follow orders, set off for an isolated corner and started digging in one of the least promising spots. Elliot had a sixth sense, however disastrous the scrapes it led him into. Within 15 minutes he had unearthed the lid of a clay pot. Nobody was looking when he lifted it off to find the crumbled remains of a skull inside.

Its owner had clearly been killed by a blow of tremendous force, landing on the right hemisphere. Elliot also noticed something else: the eye socket and the cheekbone had become separated from the upper jaw, and there was a bronze ring hooked into the nasal sinus.

Elliot placed this curiosity in his jacket pocket before calling Bill over to inspect his find. From that day on Elliot kept the bone on his fireplace mantel as a conversation piece. A few months after the discovery, his Florida house burned down and the insurance company's compensation fell short of his loss.

Elliot had received repeated warnings. On one occasion an Indian sitar player, who was a friend of his, arrived at the house with a Tibetan monk. The monk looked at the skull in horror.

"Get it out of here," he implored. "You must rebury it with a proper appeasement."

Elliot laughed.

"What on earth for?" he inquired scornfully.

"It has terrific power, and it feels a sense of outrage towards you. It doesn't like being exposed as an object of ridicule."

"Explain something to me. I don't understand the significance of this ring piercing the bone."

"He was an immensely powerful shaman," the monk frowned. "He inserted the ring himself, once he'd reached a certain level of mastery. Every time he gave it a twist, the accumulated verdigris poisoned his bloodstream, giving rise to visions. It was his means of getting in touch with heaven or hell."

"Wonderful," murmured Elliot, and from then on he referred to his find as "my pet shaman."

Marcia jotted down: "Anabel is radiant" in her book of notes on the resident foreigners. At last she had found happiness. "Who would have thought it?" she kept repeating. "Paris, Rome, Mexico and it turns out to be here, in this tiny lost village of Deyá, that I've found what I've always been looking for."

The source of Anabel's happiness was a young Indian, a teacher of Tantric yoga, who had aroused her kundalini serpent and was on the point of opening her fourth chakra. Indiri had taught her to enjoy sensual pleasure to its fullest extent. Eating an apple, drinking a fine wine, making love, everything was different now, and still they'd only gotten as far as the fourth chakra.

After fifteen months of utter bliss, Indiri informed her that he had to return to Calcutta so that his guru could open his sixth and seventh chakras.

Anabel, in the meantime, had been selling her apartment in Paris and buying a little house in Deyá. This she filled with thick white carpets and brilliantly colored cushions, and she began to give Hatha yoga classes which Marcia attended. During the four months Indiri was in Calcutta, Anabel — utterly out of character — was totally faithful to him.

At long last the day of his return arrived. Indiri landed in Palma on the 6 p.m. flight. He was more beautiful than ever. Anabel trembled with emotion at the sight of him and ran to give him a kiss. She found him changed; he virtually avoided her lips. No doubt he was tired. When they got home Anabel, with shining eyes, began kissing him again, and offered him a Bloody Mary, his favorite drink.

"Count me out," he said, "I've given up drinking."

"That seems very wise to me. Alcohol makes men impotent. Are you hungry?"

"Sit down," said Indiri, reclining on one of the cushions scattered about the floor.

Anabel sat down next to him, took hold of one of his hands and gazed deeply into his eyes.

"When I reached Calcutta my former guru told me he could no longer teach me, that he'd send me on to one with even greater wisdom. He's an extraordinary man, Anabel; he has changed my life."

Anabel listened with bated breath.

"Did he open your seventh chakra?"

"Yes," Indiri smiled, "and I'm the happiest man on earth. I've renounced everything: drink, music, the ways of the flesh. Everything."

Elliot always attracted accidents, but this year the small disasters that had long buzzed around him multiplied. What brought everything to a blazing climax was his purchase of the boat.

Elliot had an unusual obsession. Ever since he wrote his doctoral thesis on *Beowulf,* he dreamt of going to the Baltic Sea on an expedition of submarine exploration, in order to locate the grave of his hero.

One day the opportunity arose for him to buy the boat that once belonged to Jessica Brown's late ex-husband and he hastened to do so. He paid by check and only later discovered that its two diesel motors needed to be totally overhauled. Weeks later, the deceased's mistress appeared flourishing a holographic will, in which it was made known that the departed had left her the boat and an apartment in Palma. As a final aggravation, Jessica had sold off his mooring right at the Yacht Club without bothering to inform Elliot.

As soon as he realized this, Elliot, in a fit of rage, wrote Jessica Brown's name three times on separate pieces of paper and, under the eyeless stare of the shaman, howled: "I curse you, I curse you, I curse you," as he threw the pieces of paper into the fire one by one.

One stormy night a week later Jessica was in her house, alone except for the parrot and her Ibizan dog, when she heard a rapping of knuckles on the Venetian blinds.

"Who is it?" she asked.

The reply came in the form of an insidious laugh.

She picked up an axe with shaking hands and went through the house making sure that all the doors and windows were securely locked. She heard a sound in the kitchen and returned on tiptoe. Through the window she could see a gloved hand removing one of the slats of the shutters. She opened the casement and struck out at the hand. There was a howl and it disappeared. She put on all the lights in the house and waited, rooted to the floor in terror, the axe in her hand. A few minutes later she heard a noise in her bedroom, as if the marauder were attempting to force the window at the back of the house. Without further ado, Jessica fled through the front door in her nightdress and a few seconds later, crazed with fright, was hammering on the door of the fishermen's house. She spent the night with them. Tomás and Pedro went the next morning to check over her house and found a man's footprints in the mud.

The next night Jessica went to stay at Stephen's house. In the small hours she got up feeling dizzy, and made her way to the bathroom. She missed her step and tumbled all the way down a flight of stairs onto the stone floor, breaking her right arm and smashing one side of her face.

When Slim and Marcia moved into Ca'n Blau, the renovation was still incomplete. Slim, who was something of a jack of all trades and interested in everything, worked hard alongside the workmen. The whole ground floor and staircase were as yet unfinished, but the bedrooms and bathroom were usable. Marcia woke before dawn. In spite of the darkness she could easily discern a shape kneeling by the door. She sat up in bed and screamed, digging her nails in Slim's arm as he snored blissfully beside her.

"Who are you? What are you doing here?"

"What?" Slim's voice was thick with sleep.

"He's bowing his head again," Marcia's voice trembled.

Slim sat up in bed and put an arm around her. "You're dreaming. There's no one there."

"How come you can't see anything? There he is, he's very tall." Marcia's body was rigid. Slim was unable to make out anything, anything at all.

"Put on the light," she pleaded.

Slim, still half-asleep yet seriously alarmed, slid out of the bed, fell over a chair in the middle of the unfamiliar room and passed through the phantom to switch on the light.

"See? Nobody here."

"He was there until you put the light on. He had his head bowed, lifted it when I addressed him, then dropped it again."

Slim sighed and sat down on the edge of the bed. "What was he like?"

"Extremely tall and thin. He couldn't have been more than twenty-five. His head was all shaven and he wore long underwear like my grandfather's."

"Did he wear shoes?"

"I couldn't tell. I didn't see his feet."

"What was he doing?"

"Nothing. He looked up when I spoke to him, then his head dropped again."

Slim got back into bed and Marcia wrapped herself around him like a quivering octopus.

"Aren't you going to turn out the light?" she asked.

"First I'm going to smoke a cigarette." He freed an arm to reach for the pack and lighter on the bedside table.

"Look, Marcia," he said after two or three drags, "we shouldn't say a word about this to anyone."

"But it was terrifying!"

"You were afraid because you imagined there was a thief in the house," Slim consoled her. "There was nothing to be afraid of. In any case ghosts are as harmless as cats."

"Cats frighten me too," she reminded him. She remained silent a moment before adding: "I'll ask Uncle Juan if a tall thin boy died in this room."

Uncle Juan lived in Francisca's house, which was really his but he'd given to her on condition she looked after him and washed his feet until the day he died.

"Better not," said Slim. "Francisca would make it her business to inform the entire village. If you want I can bring it up with Pepe. It'd be interesting to know whether Ca'n Blau has a reputation for being haunted. Maybe that's why we got it so cheap."

"Some bargain if we have to share it with generations of ghosts! Uncle Juan said it had been empty for seventy years when we bought it."

Suddenly Slim struck his forehead with the flat of his hand. "What an idiot I am! Do you realize what night it is?"

"No."

"It's St. John's Eve, stupid. We were at the fiesta until half-past midnight."

"And what has that got to do with it?"

"It's the celebration of the summer solstice, when ghosts make their appearance all over Europe. If we're lucky ours will only pay us a visit once a year."

"Then next year you can be sure I'll spend the night in a hotel."

"Fine," Slim gave her a kiss. "But it's important to say nothing of this to anyone, not even Pepe. You know how rumors run rampant here. Whatever happened to us would be on everyone else's lips inside of half an hour. With luck our ghost will only have the energy to turn up on St. John's Eve, but if the whole village starts feeding it gossip, it'll gain enough strength to come and keep pestering us all the time."

"You're right, but I don't see what harm it'd do to put an innocuous question to Uncle Juan."

Slim didn't reply. He put out his cigarette, extricated himself from Marcia's embrace, and got up to put out the light again.

Three days later Jerry Preston entered Ca'n Blau without bothering to knock on the door. It was lunchtime. Slim was away in Palma, and Marcia, who had mentioned absolutely nothing to anyone of what had happened, was making a ham and cheese sandwich for herself.

"Can you make one for me too?" Jerry inquired. She agreed, and started another for him.

She hardly knew Jerry. She'd only heard of him as one of the last authentic hippies. He lived in the ruined tower at the far end of Punta Deyá and, like so many others during that period, spent a large part of the time stoned.

"Let's go to the terrace," Marcia suggested. "Everything down here is in chaos."

They went upstairs without talking and sat down in the shade. Jerry gulped down his sandwich voraciously, took a large gulp of Coca Cola and cleared his throat.

"I came to tell you that what you saw the other night was an angel. It didn't mean to frighten or harm you."

Marcia shivered but she refrained from saying anything. She stared at him attentively for a few moments.

No, it definitely hadn't been him. Jerry had flowing locks and was short.

"Besides," he continued, "this house has good vibes and is well protected. In any case, just to make sure I'll fumigate it."

He said goodbye, only to reappear two hours later with a bunch of white flowers in his hand.

"Do you have any tacks?" he asked.

"I think so. Just a minute."

Despite the untidiness reigning in the house, Marcia found a box of thumbtacks and handed it to him. Jerry got up on a chair and solemnly began to tack flowers over the doorway and above both window frames.

"Periwinkles," deduced Marcia.

"That's right. Extremely effective at keeping evil spirits at bay and against the Evil Eye."

They climbed to the other two floors and repeated the operation at each of the windows in the bedrooms and Slim's studio.

"Done," he pronounced with satisfaction, "your house is now proof against anything."

Marcia could no longer contain her curiosity. "Why did you tell me it was an angel?"

"Because I could see how worried you were. I'll call back another day, it's getting late."

As soon as she got out of the hospital, Jessica sold up and left for California where her daughter lived, never to return to this "accursed place." No one ever discovered who her attacker had been. Some suspected Elliot because whenever he got drunk he told the most horrible stories about her. But Elliot had spent that night in the Café Deportivo in Fornalutx, getting drunk with friends.

Others suspected Tony de las Cabras. On separate occasions two women living alone on the outskirts of Deyá had been beaten and raped by a hooded man who left them gagged and tied to the bedposts. People muttered against Tony who'd been acting peculiarly ever since Ben died, but there was insufficient evidence against him.

A few days after Jessica departed, Elliot turned up in Deyá one afternoon riding a Vespa. He came into Ca'n Blau trembling with fear, to question Slim and Marcia about what had happened to Jessica. He was already half drunk and poured himself a couple of stiff whiskies to see him through his confession of the curse he'd placed on Jessica.

"You fool," Slim told him. "You don't play around with things like that."

Elliot defended himself. "It was in a fit of rage. I never dreamt anything so awful could result."

Finally he calmed down a little. "I've got to leave," he said, getting up.

"Why don't you spend the night here?" Marcia offered. "It's started raining and the road must be very slippery."

"I can't. I need to be alone to think through all this stuff."

"Be careful," Marcia warned him.

At noon the following day, Elliot again appeared in the doorway of Ca'n Blau and on seeing his face Marcia let out a scream. His right cheekbone was shattered and a bloody eye was bulging out of its socket.

"What happened, Elliot?"

"The Vespa slipped out of control on the climb to Fornalutx and I went over the edge with it. I was unconscious for several hours but I finally managed to crawl up to the highway and some kindly soul took me to a doctor."

"Come in, come in," said Marcia. "Do you want me to make you a cup of tea?"

"I can't stay, the taxi's waiting outside for me. I only came to say goodbye. I've booked myself on a flight for London. It leaves in an hour and a half. They filled me up with novocaine and I'll have to be operated on as soon as possible, in order not to lose the sight in my right eye."

He returned a month later, in the company of a blonde nurse he'd bewitched during his convalescence. Slim and Marcia found him in Stephen's house. His face no longer looked the same. It had a pronounced asymmetry. He was taciturn and didn't burst into chatter as he used to.

"What's the best way for me to rid myself of the shaman?" he asked Stephen, taking the bone out of his pocket.

"I'll have to think it over and check out some references," Stephen answered. "But in the meantime I don't want you to leave it lying around in my house."

Some days later Elliot, the nurse and Stephen went to the cave underneath Son Rullan and reburied the skull in the same place from which it had been disinterred. After the ceremony Elliot and the blonde stopped by at Ca'n Blau and Elliot provided the details of the rites to Slim and Marcia.

According to Elliot, Stephen had fallen into a trance while offering up prayers of appeasement. He had begun to babble incoherently while copious tears flowed down his cheeks. Finally he came out of his trance and the three of them deposited sprays of periwinkles on the little grave.

That night Marcia had a dream. In it a little old man dressed in goatskin came to her and said: "I've changed my mind. I no longer like my old burial ground, it's too noisy around there." Marcia observed that hooked in his cheek, below his right eye, he wore a bronze ring.

"Who are you?"

"My name is Sea Eagle and I want you to take me somewhere else."

Marcia awoke with a start. It was six in the morning. She lay rigid in bed, eyes wide open, for another half hour, struggling to decipher the dream. She got up quietly to avoid waking Slim and went down to the kitchen to make herb tea. As she sipped it, she decided what she must do.

At around seven o'clock she left Ca'n Blau, taking her little rake and the trowel she used for her window boxes in her basket. She walked to the car parked in front of Bill Waldren's house and drove to Son Rullan. It was hard work finding the path leading down from the lowest terrace to the cavern, but as soon as she arrived she spotted Sea Eagle's grave decorated with periwinkles. She dug up the casket, filled the hole again and put the flowers, already withering, back on top.

It was eight o'clock when she reached the village. She parked the car in front of the Waldrens' house again and, without an instant's hesitation, climbed up the narrow steps to Ca'n Oliver. There she took the familiar path to the tree that had been hers now for several months, excavated a hole between two protruding roots and deposited the casket in it. Before covering it over with earth she said aloud: "Sea Eagle, here you have a splendid view and complete solitude. May you rest in peace."

When she stood up she dusted her hands and looked towards the Teix where she saw the Foradada eagle describing figures of eight in the sky, and she was certain that this was the sign: the old shaman was well pleased with his new home.

The night of the wake for Miguel's father next door to Ca'n Blau, Marcia met up with the corpse-dresser again.

"Bon día," she greeted her.

"Bon día," Marcia answered. "Always working, isn't that so?"

"That's right," the old woman agreed. "Since I turned twenty I've been dressing the dead and now I'm over seventy. You can figure it out for yourself."

"Would you like a cup of coffee?"

"I wouldn't mind."

Marcia got up to pour one, then the two of them went to sit down in a corner of the dining room.

"Do you know something?" the dresser looked at Marcia with tenderness. "Up until now I've only dressed Mallorcans, but I've taken a liking to you, and I'm going to dress you too."

Marcia smiled timidly but couldn't quite bring herself to say thank you. She could feel her hands trembling.

"In this job you get to learn a lot about people," the dresser continued.

"I can imagine."

"Miguel's father, for example. You know that when his wife fell ill years ago, he decided to climb into bed with her and there was no way of getting him up again. When she died a year later he got up as though nothing had happened. He lasted another ten years after that."

Marcia burst out laughing.

163

"But the strangest thing," the old woman's eyes lit up, "the weirdest thing of all that only the old folk like myself remember was what happened to Manuela. You don't know who Manuela was, do you?"

Marcia shook her head.

"She came from one of the poorest families, all the rest of them boys. When she was born the whole village celebrated. After all those boys — six of them I think — her mother was longing for a girl. Manuela was hideous and nobody really liked her. When she was about twenty-five they married her to Bernardo, the village idiot. Bernardo was a good and docile man, an only son. He came from a well-off family, the owners of Ca'n Calafat. All those terraces belonged to them.

"Poor Bernardo, he always fancied pretty girls, but none of them ever took any notice of him. His parents grew worried; they didn't want him to stay a bachelor and they married him off to Manuela. They died soon after and Bernardo and Manuela moved into Ca'n Calafat.

"Early each morning the two of them went to work out on the terraces. Manuela would sit down under a pear tree and issue orders to Bernardo. They never had children. They were an isolated pair, they hardly saw anyone else. Manuela never bothered to visit her brothers, even though she was the spoiled youngster of the family. They lived like that for about thirty years.

"One day Bernardo turned up at the home of the fisherman's family and told them he was worried. Manuela, always such an early bird, didn't want to get up. The fisherman and his wife ran to the house. When they explained to Bernardo that his wife had died, he collapsed in a fit of uncontrollable sobbing. The neighbors had to take over and manage everything, even going to Sóller to buy a coffin.

"I arrived there shortly before dinnertime, went up to the bedroom — and came straight down again, my legs shaking. I told three of my women friends who were waiting there to come up with me. They did, frightened to see me in such a state.

Manuela was lying covered with a sheet. "Please — tell me if you see what I see," I asked, and pulled back the sheet.

"Manuela, who'd died at the age of fifty-five, turned out to have been a Manuel."

Jerry paid another visit to Ca'n Blau, at lunchtime as usual. Slim was at home. Marcia made an extra sandwich and the three of them went upstairs to the terrace.

"How on earth did you know we'd seen a ghost?" Slim asked Jerry. "We never said a word to anyone."

"What are you talking about?" Jerry asked in surprise. "Did you really see a ghost?"

Slim got impatient. "Are you denying that you turned up at the house three days ago to tell Marcia that what she'd seen was an angel? That it wasn't you who nailed all those periwinkles up over the windows?"

"Me?" Jerry sounded incredulous. "I did all that? When?"

"Monday," replied Marcia. "Monday at midday."

"Ah," said Jerry. "On Monday I overdosed on acid and was out of my head the whole day. Can't remember a thing about it."

Slim and Marcia looked at each other in astonishment.

"But last night," Jerry mused, "I had a really important dream. I dreamt that Robert was dressed like Zeus, king of the Greek gods, and that I was employed to work as a kind of messenger for him."

"Hermes," replied Slim, who was half-way through one of Robert's two volumes of Greek mythology.

"Precisely," said Jerry, "that's it. Robert called me up to his house and scolded me fiercely because, according to him, I had been talking too much and neglecting my duties."

Slim's clear and rational mind — despite his experience of enlightenment — would have been deeply perturbed by Jerry's extraordinary behavior, had it not been for Robert, who cleared up the incident. At that time, Slim and Marcia scarcely knew Robert. They'd only spoken to him once before when he passed by the house as they were leaning out of one of the bedroom windows; he was wearing shorts and a wide-brimmed straw hat, a Deyá basket hanging from his shoulder.

"How I'd love to talk to him," Marcia whispered to Slim. "He must be a fascinating person."

Robert paused. He looked up at the window and said "good morning." Overjoyed, Marcia invited him in.

"Thank you," said Robert, tossing a ping-pong ball into the air and catching it again. "Did you buy this house?"

"Yes," Slim answered. "We've really taken to the village."

"That's good, that's good," Robert answered, "I'll come and visit you again another day," and he set off down the road with long strides and disappeared around the corner.

The same night that Jerry returned to visit them they met up with Robert in Ca'n Quet. He was having dinner with Mel, a gifted astrologer who could also read palms. Slim told Robert about what had happened.

"That boy must be clairvoyant," concluded Robert. "What a pity about all the drug-taking." Then he turned to Marcia: "Tell me about the man who appeared to you. You say his head was shaved. Did he have sideburns?"

"Yes, and I particularly noticed them because despite his baldness, they were very pronounced."

"His nose was large and flattened?"

"Yes," Marcia was increasingly surprised.

"Aha," grunted Robert, "then it was Ted Murphy. A nasty murderer who lived around here until two years ago."

"When did he die?" asked Slim.

"He's not dead," Robert's voice didn't waver. "He lives in the United States. He killed a friend of mine who lived close by the Cala. He's a terrible person."

"But if he's alive, how could Marcia have seen his ghost?" asked Slim.

"The living project ghosts just like the dead," replied Robert. "It's simply a matter of gathering sufficient energy."

It was a cold December day, one of those when the interminable clouds over Valdemossa stretch and expand to cover even Deyá.

Marcia was returning from doing the shopping accompanied by Bobby, her white, woolly dog with the golden eyes who was more a *cadejo** than a real dog, when suddenly — and in the middle of the road — they encountered the same girl that only the other day Bobby had approached, sniffed, lifted his leg and peed on.

Marcia had been deeply embarrassed, and had apologized profusely. The girl had just sat there staring motionlessly. Now Marcia stopped to survey her. What was she doing in the middle of the highway?

The girl, who was French and couldn't have been more than twenty years old, was concentrating on cutting up strips of adhesive bandages. Marcia approached her slowly. Without getting up, Colette cut a large strip and placed it over a crack in the asphalt.

"What are you doing?" Marcia asked her. "It's dangerous to sit here."

Colette looked up indifferently. In her own way she was healing the wounds of the world.

While Stephen was waiting outside the vegetable lady's shop to receive his change from Catalina's long, slender fingers, his eyes lit on Catalina's niece who was just emerging from the shop peeling a banana. The girl paused to close the door, dropped the peel on the pavement and ran over to her friends munching the banana.

Stephen eyed the peel as though it were a cobra, took the change blindly and headed for the door without shifting his gaze. He stopped, rooted to the ground at the sight of Slim, who was just getting out of his car which was parked opposite the

---

* *Cadejo*: spirit of a native Central American dog, bringing good or bad luck, depending on the color.

167

vegetable store. Slim crossed the street and picked up the banana skin.

"Aha!" Stephen announced. "Caught you."

Slim straightened up, surprised. "What's that?"

"Why did you pick up that banana peel?" Stephen asked.

"I thought someone might slip on it. What's wrong with that?"

"Stop it Slim, don't spin me any tales. Come with me right away."

"I can't, Stephen. I've got to work."

"No excuses. You and I are going to have a talk."

Slim let himself be led by the arm to the corner, then up the hill to Stephen's house.

"What's going on?" he asked. "Have you gone crazy?"

"You know perfectly well what's going on. We'll talk when we get home."

Stephen opened the front door and nodded towards one of the chairs at the table where he always served tea. "Sit down and don't move," he ordered. "I'll be back in a moment."

He went upstairs, returning a few minutes later with a voluminous black notebook. He placed it on the table and sat down opposite Slim.

"Now tell me truthfully: why did you pick up the banana peel?"

"To avoid a possible accident."

Stephen folded his hands, resting them on the black notebook.

"For years I've had the feeling that I'm only a minor character in a novel written by someone else. All the deeds of my unfortunate life do nothing but confirm this impression and I've taken a vow to revenge myself on the author as soon as I meet him."

"What?"

"You can't fool me. I've got proof. You and your damned definitive novel about Deyá."

"For God's sake," Slim sighed. "What's your proof?"

"I'll begin at the beginning. Three nights ago, as you'll remember, I dropped by at Ca'n Blau before dinnertime and hung my basket on the coat hook in the kitchen as usual. As I left I took yours by mistake and didn't notice it until I got home. I . . . I have to confess" — now he was stammering — "that I opened your notebook to make absolutely certain that it was your basket. What I read so appalled me that very early the next day I went into Ca'n Blau while Francisca was washing dishes and you were both still asleep. I returned your basket and recovered my own."

"A gentleman would never read a diary belonging to someone else," Slim exploded.

"I beg your pardon," said Stephen, "but the misdeed was more than justified. How are you going to explain this to me?"

He opened the black notebook and read aloud: "July 23 — Poor old Stephen had a bad fall this morning in front of the vegetable shop. He slipped on a banana peel and lay stretched on the ground with a concussion and scalp wounds. Marcia and I just went to visit him in the clinic at Son Dureta, and the poor fellow is even crazier than usual."

"Do you have anything to say?" Stephen looked at Slim again. Slim searched in vain for words.

"What date is it today?" Stephen insisted.

"Hard to tell," said Slim. "One loses track of the days here."

"Not so," Stephen replied. "You know perfectly well that today is the 23rd of July."

"You're right," Slim agreed. "Tomorrow is Robert's birthday."

"How can it be," Stephen resumed his interrogation, "that on the 20th or thereabouts you were taking notes dated the 23rd?"

"Coincidence?" suggested Slim timidly.

"There's no such thing as coincidence," replied Stephen. "On the 20th you knew perfectly well what was going to happen to me today, only fifteen minutes ago."

"As you wish," Slim's voice was weary. "But you have to admit that I spent the whole blessed morning sitting in my car waiting for a child to chuck a banana peel on to the pavement. I picked it up to save your neck."

"Many thanks for your kindness. I'm forced to concede that maybe you didn't wish to kill me, but I beg you, Slim, in the future not to involve me in any other near-fatal accidents and, if at all possible, try to treat my humble person with a little more respect. I'd like to retain at least the semblance of dignity."

"I don't understand you, Stephen."

"You're writing the story of my life," Stephen leaned across the table. "If you carry on playing around like this, I regret to inform you that it'll cut short our friendship."

"It's not what you think," Slim sounded resigned. "I swear that I'm not playing around with your life, nor do I have the least desire to do so. I consider you a real friend and have a lot of respect for you. What's happened is this: several years ago when we were living in Paris, I had a transcendental experience, which went on for so long that the psychiatrist had to treat me with electric shock therapy. A whole series of intensive electric shocks. The treatment was virtually one hundred per cent effective, but it burned out not only the memory of my transcendental experiences but also almost every memory of my past. The worst part of it all is that it left me with a larger-than-normal time window."

"What's this about time windows?"

"It's a bit complicated. Everyone takes it for granted that one lives in the present and that life's events unfold naturally from now into the future, squarely focusing on the present and sliding off again into what we are pleased to call the past. As I was saying, my window is simply considerably wider than what most people look through. I undergo frequent lapses that take me anywhere from three days to a week into the past or the future."

"Are you serious?" Stephen opened wide his sky-blue eyes.

"Yes. And I freely admit — as an example — how boring it is to relive a dinner in dull company a second time around. However, that doesn't matter too much, since I can keep it under control: I retain the memory of the first occasion, and remember that I've been through it all before. Slipping into the future is a far trickier matter. I'm always convinced that I'm still living in the present moment and that everyone around me also takes it as being exactly the same *now*. As a rule it's only when things start happening for the second time around that I become aware of the fact that I've been through another time-warp. Of course it's unpleasant, but it seems to be something that doesn't only happen to me but to lots of people. They call it different things — *déjà vu*, clairvoyance, precognition, what you will."

"How fascinating," Stephen's voice had dropped to a whisper. "I believe you, Slim, and I apologize."

"Do you really believe me?" Slim was surprised. "I've never spoken of this to anyone apart from Marcia. Everyone would think I was crazy and I detest the idea of having to undergo electric shock treatment a second time."

"I promise you I do believe you, Slim. I know of another case similar to yours, except that the time-warps lasted much longer."

"Really?" Slim was intrigued. "Who was it?"

"Raimundo Lulio, the Mallorcan philosopher and alchemist. I never knew him personally, but Robert did."

"Raimundo Lulio?" Slim sounded perplexed. "But Lulio died hundreds of years ago."

"I know. In 1316 to be precise. As I was telling you, he could cross the time barrier into the future. Robert held some truly fascinating conversations with him. He wrote them down in an unpublished manuscript that happened to fall into my hands."

"Incredible. Robert never mentioned any of this to me."

"I know. The truth is that he doesn't really remember it. It occurred during the period when he'd started work on *The White Goddess*. And he always insists that he'd spent the entire period in an altered state of consciousness."

"I know what you mean. Go on, tell me the whole story."

"Certainly," said Stephen enthusiastically, "but it's somewhat long and my throat's getting dry. I'll put some water on to boil while I start telling you."

Slim settled back in his chair and Stephen began his story en route to the kitchen.

"I came across the manuscript *Conversations with Raimundo Lulio* in a secret compartment of my old desk in our country house. This must have been about a year before I came to Deyá. My father was a great friend of Robert's and, following the bombing of the Graves' London apartment during the last war, invited him and Beryl out to share our house. It was there Robert wrote *The White Goddess.*

"I didn't see them at all throughout this period. I was in the United States, working on the atomic bomb. Do you remember it, the famous Manhattan project? After the war I worked at Harwell for a long time, helping to make sure the thing worked. My special skills were in nuclear metallurgy, and devouring books on astrophysics became a hobby for me. An ideally tranquil way of life for a bachelor.

"Suddenly one day there was a slow pressure drop in the cooling system and I went to see what was going on. Looking through a window with leaded panes, I discovered a flaw: an infinitesimal crack in the main circulation pipe. A pall of radioactive vapor was escaping through it and growing by the minute. I dashed in without putting on protective clothing. There simply wasn't time to do so. I opened the escape valve, closed down the principal system and got the hell out, yelling at everyone around not to come near me without covering themselves.

"As you can see, the radiation dose wasn't fatal. I lost my hair and my teeth began falling out. A wig and a dental plate dealt with those problems, but the worst of it was that my mind began skidding. No one could do anything to help. They decided to retire me with industrial accident compensation. A hundred pounds a month.

"One day I went back to the country house and was shuffling through papers in my room when I remembered the secret compartment in the desk. That was when I came across the manuscript that Robert had obviously forgotten there.

"It all took place in Deyá a few years before the outbreak of the Civil War. According to Robert, Lulio simply materialized at noon one day in his study and began interrogating him in archaic Catalan. It's not Robert's strongest language so Lulio soon switched to Latin.

"It turned out that Lulio was looking for the philosophers' stone that had vanished 659 years earlier, and wanted to know if Robert could locate it for him. Robert said no, he didn't know anything about it. 'But it's got to be somewhere around here,' rumbled the old philosopher. 'I always turn up in its vicinity.' He told him that for years he'd been repeatedly tossed between past and future, always hoping to find himself in 1276 and on the path to his monastery at Miramar, Mallorca.

"Lulio became very worried when Robert let him know that it was now 1935 and that Deyá was only a few miles away from his Miramar monastery. 'I've almost made it to the right place, but the time is still all wrong,' he said sadly. 'It's the closest I've come until now. Please take me there. Perhaps I'll be able to discover something.' Robert had to accompany him to Miramar. As they walked along the dirt road leading to Valdemossa, Lulio asked Robert if he knew of any inexplicable happenings that had recently taken place in Deyá. 'To be honest,' Robert replied, 'strange things are always happening here in this village of God. Without doubt, it must be one of the most mysterious places in the world.'

'Then the stone can't be far away,' Lulio was warming to his subject. 'You can't imagine all the exotic places I've been to recently: Babylonia, Uttar Pradesh, Lhasa, the Forbidden City, Delphos, the Pyramids, Atlantis, Solomon's Mines. You can keep the lot of them.' They paused by the Archduke's palace at Son Marroig, and looked out over La Muleta and the Teix wall. 'The landscape hasn't changed,' said Lulio. He waved in the direction of Sa Foradada and indicated the gigantic Cyclopean

173

eye in the stone sea monster emerging from the Mediterranean. 'Mahomet and I made that when we manufactured the philosophers' stone,' he announced with satisfaction.

Robert stared at him incredulously.

'Mahomet,' Lulio explained, 'was a Sufi smith who disguised himself as a servant while he became my teacher of Arabic and the Great Art and initiated me into the enigmatic writings of Al Ghazali, around the year 1274. An extremely wise man. He told me that Al Khidr (the Archangel Michael, you know) had chosen me to serve as his assistant in the fabrication of the philosophers' stone. It made me very happy, me a humble Franciscan monk living there on an island lost in the middle of the Mediterranean. Why had he chosen me? I asked myself. I soon discovered it was because I had a strong back. Manufacturing the stone required the stamina of a coal miner, and was as dirty as it was hard. We had to excavate and transport tons of sand and gravel daily.'

'But to return to the subject of the hole, we got to the point where the philosophers' stone was devouring more matter than we could manage to feed into it, and it still wasn't stabilizing. We had to immobilize it with magnets. We carried it to the summit of Sa Foradada and suspended it from a jib crane with a pulley at the end. We lowered it down the slope and let it gnaw away at the rock. It was feeding itself. All that was left for us to do was to sit there, moving the arm of the crane backwards and forwards from time to time and lowering the rope as it fed.

'It took us about a month to clear the whole area and come out the other side. It must have gobbled up fifty thousand tons of stone. Mahomet came down one day and watched it burning the rock. He applied mercury and hydrochloric acid to it and told me it was turning the right color. We reeled it in and took it to the beach. Mahomet attached it to a cord at the end of a fishing rod and submerged it in the water. As the stone went down it created a whirlpool that soon transformed itself into a smooth tunnel some six feet deep with a blue spark at the bottom. The quay shook beneath our feet and the force of the rotating whirlpool was such that it threatened to sweep everything away, but Mahomet controlled it from above with such skill that he prevented the tunnel from growing too wide. After three hours he lifted it up for an inspection and decided that it had finally stabilized. When I looked I could see that this was indeed true. The stone had vanished and only its force remained.'"

Stephen returned from the kitchen with the teapot, cups, toast, butter and a pot of homemade jam. "Are you aware of the implications of this story, Slim?" he asked.

"I can't say I am," Slim was busily spreading butter on a slice of toast.

"What Lulio described to Robert was the behavior of a miniature black hole."

"You don't mean it . . ." Slim was so taken aback he forgot to add the jam before taking a bite of his toast.

"I assume you know what I mean by a black hole."

"Of course," Slim was quick to assure him, "it's a sun which has burnt out and implodes to vanishing point, but its gravitational mass is so strong that not even light can escape. That's why it's invisible. It also swallows up everything in its magnetic field."

"That's right," approved Stephen, stirring his tea. "Do you see it now? Lulio's description fits perfectly. They fed the black hole tons of matter and sea water until it could achieve stability within temporal coordinates. In other words, it became an atemporal object."

Stephen replaced his cup on the table. "And there's something else," he was looking deep into Slim's eyes, "Robert's manuscript contains precise instructions on the manufacture of a black hole. He helped Lulio to make one and retained notes on every stage of its construction."

"Fantastic!" Slim exclaimed. "And you possess this secret?"

Stephen pursed his lips and nodded.

"Do you have the manuscript with you? I'd love to have a look at it."

Stephen hesitated a moment before answering.

"Unfortunately I can't satisfy your curiosity. Only a nuclear metallurgist or a student of astrophysics could understand the awesome responsibility I have in my hands. It's a question of the salvation of humanity."

"I understand." Slim was disappointed. "If the secret were spread around, it could become an enormously powerful weapon."

"No, Slim. If a black hole escapes the electromagnetic charges that immobilize it, it would destroy our planet within a few weeks, at most."

"How?"

"It would fall to the earth's center and continue growing while it fed on the lithosphere and then on the magma. Finally it would consume the whole nucleus of molten nickel and metal. During those last days there would be unprecedented earthquakes and volcanic activity. The continental plates would crash into one another, vast tidal waves would devastate coastal cities and violent storms and hurricanes would sweep the planet. Barely a handful of people would survive to experience the ultimate physical enigma: to be swallowed into the jaws of a black hole."

Slim was intrigued by Stephen's story about the philosophers' stone. He arrived home late for lunch and recounted it all to Marcia from beginning to end.

"It seems to me that the manuscript found by Stephen was nothing more than a short story Robert wrote and forgot about after he started work on *The White Goddess,*" was Marcia's opinion.

Slim contradicted her: "No, you don't know all the details. Stephen told me he'd been working unsuccessfully for a year in his country house in England, trying to reproduce the philosophers' stone with the help of the formula he found in the manuscript. Finally, in despair, he flew out to Mallorca to ask Robert what he was doing wrong. Robert only sighed heavily. "My dear friend," he told him, "it's obvious that to create the philosophers' stone, in the first place one must be a philosopher and in the second, in a state of grace. Next, you were working in the wrong place. The stone is here in Deyá and you have to create propitious conditions in order to draw it out of atemporality and into your alchemical kiln."

"Robert's manuscript tells how Lulio offered his help to mount the apparatus and attract the stone from out of the interdimensional ether. It cost them several weeks of hard work, despite the fact that they did not have to carry the quantities of sand and gravel Lulio and Mahomet did on the first occasion. It was Robert's suggestion that they use an acetylene torch as the most efficient source of heat. They obtained the necessary chemical products from some industrial suppliers and chemists in Palma. When they finished the process and the stone was caught in the electromagnetic field, Lulio thanked Robert for his help and told him: 'Right, I hope that this time it works out.' Robert said yes, of course. 'After all, we consulted the *Encyclopaedia Britannica* and found that you reappeared in Miramar in 1287 to continue your long and fruitful life to its end in 1316.'

'Then it's best for me to leave now,' replied Lulio, and without another word he put his finger into the electro-magnetic cage. His arm stretched interminably and in the wink of an eye he had shrunk to vanishing point.'"

"And what happened to the stone?" asked Marcia.

"Stephen asked Robert the same question. Robert said that he'd studied it for a while but that it never did anything but swallow everything you fed it and want more. As he had no intention of putting his index finger into the cage in order to go on a time trip like Lulio, he left it somewhere safe so it couldn't start gobbling up the earth and forgot about it. This whole episode of the manuscript and the stone was erased from his memory with the outbreak of the Spanish Civil War and the preparations for his sudden return to England."

"But it's near Robert's house; I know where to look for it," said Marcia.

"What?" Slim looked at her in amazement.

"It must be in the magic garden. Lulio said that weird things were always happening in its vicinity."

"Come with me," Slim dragged her to her feet, "Stephen must hear about this."

"Marcia says that the philosophers' stone is in Robert's magic garden," Slim announced triumphantly.

"Sit down, sit down," said Stephen, "I'll have finished slicing the bread in a minute. What's all this about a magic garden?"

"Don't you know about it?" asked Marcia. "It's behind Robert's house. He walled it in years ago. He had to put it in quarantine after the plants started going crazy."

"Strange how he never mentioned any of this to me," Stephen frowned.

"He hates the whole business and refuses to discuss it. He was proud of his green thumb and took it as a personal affront. He even decided to secure the gate with a padlock. One day, in a bad mood, he took me for a walk and showed it to me."

"Tell me about it." Stephen's anxiety was mounting.

"It all began before he left for England. One year he planted potato seed and what do you think he harvested? Five tons of beets. He had to feed them to the neighbors' pigs. The next year was even worse: he planted seven different kinds of vegetable and the whole garden turned into tropical jungle, full of orchids, lianas and some revolting flowers that ate insects and worms. That was when he decided to wall it in, shortly before leaving for England."

"You could be right," said Stephen, "astrophysicists have calculated that the laws of nature cease to function in the vicinity of a black hole and anything can happen. Absolutely anything."

"What's all this about black holes?" asked Marcia.

"I'll explain it later," promised Slim, "it's a highly complicated concept. Don't you think we should go and take a look?" he asked Stephen.

"Of course."

He turned off the stove where the water was boiling away in the kettle, crammed his wool hat on his head, hung a sign on the door which read "Back in half an hour" and ushered them out.

Robert didn't oppose their visiting the garden, but warned them that he had not entered the "damned place" for a good many years. He'd lost the key to the padlock.

Stephen took Robert's axe and a metal bar and they all set off for the garden behind the house.

Stephen inserted one end of the metal bar between the bolt and the padlock, handed the other end to Slim, telling him to hold on tightly, stepped back a pace and aimed a powerful blow at the crossbar. The padlock fell off and Slim let out a little yelp and shook his tingling hands.

Stephen removed the bolt, opened the gate and stared in surprise at the exuberant vegetation. With a worried expression he began examining a spiky creeper that had covered the whole area.

"Incredible, utterly incredible," he whispered.

He picked one of the little fruits. It was yellow and splotched with ochre patches. "The head hunters of Borneo use this stuff to poison their darts. It's absolutely lethal."

He let the fruit fall to the ground and examined the enclosure.

"It must be somewhere in the middle."

He gingerly set off through the prickly undergrowth towards the scarecrow in the middle of the miniature jungle. He pulled open its raggedy rain-cape and exclaimed: "Aha, this must be it!"

The rain-cape with its long sleeves was hung on a wooden cross and there was a birdcage dangling from the crossbar. Stephen unhooked it and approached the others, holding it well above the ground.

"Robert, is the philosophers' stone in here?"

"Yes. Now I remember I hung it up here while we were suffering a plague of insects in the garden. The stone swallowed them all. Let's see if it's still working."

He plucked a long stalk of grass and pushed it through the bars into the cage.

The cage seized it from his hands and swallowed it instantly.

"Hasn't changed a bit," commented Robert. "Same old useless thing."

"Would you mind a lot," Stephen was taking pains not to show his eagerness, "if I borrowed it for a few days? I'd like to undertake a few experiments to discover whether or not it's what I think it is."

"Take it away," Robert gave a shrug, "but be careful not to stick your finger between its bars or you'll be swallowed up the same as Lulio. You could find yourself in the thirteenth century, or some place where you can't even get a decent cup of tea."

"I'll be very careful," Stephen promised, "and tomorrow I'll bring you a new padlock for the gate, though I don't really believe it'll be necessary from now on."

The three of them bade Robert goodbye and began walking back to the village. Stephen kept a firm grip on the cage.

"Amazing, Slim. The first pocket-sized black hole ever to fall into mankind's possession. Just think what that means."

"What are you going to do with it?" asked Slim.

"Just a few simple experiments for the time being. I'll measure the diameter of the accretion disc and a few other things, to see if it behaves according to the astrophysicists' predictions. Why don't you come over to my house in three or four days? I think I'll have a few tangible results by then."

"Don't you remember," Bill was saying, "how the poltergeist in the Puig house turned out to be Sonny? Who'd have believed that a little kid of eleven could have kept the whole village on tenterhooks?"

"That was a child's prank," replied Marcia, "but that doesn't mean the poltergeist wasn't the originator of the previous phenomena. Remember that Robert exorcised it."

"Marcia! Don't tell me you believe all those stupid stories!"

"Why not?"

"Pure superstition," snorted Bill, "most people are still victims of the fantasies of their unconscious minds. Poltergeists never materialize in science labs."

"Of course they don't," Marcia laughed, "the atmosphere is far too cold and unsympathetic."

"Do you know Murphy's law?" Slim asked.

"No, tell us," requested Bill.

"It's a universal postulate within scientific circles. If there is the remotest possibility of a stupid mistake occurring in any experiment, then that mistake will occur."

"Another projection of the investigator's unconscious."

"What's the difference between what you call the unconscious and a poltergeist?" Marcia interposed. "I find the world a much more fascinating place if it accommo-dates poltergeists rather than a series of Freudian slips."

"As for you, Bill," said Slim, "you've never come across a poltergeist or a leprechaun because you don't believe in them and whenever they appear you simply shut your eyes. Marcia, on the other hand, discovers goblins under the bed every time she changes the sheets."

"Now that's what's called subjective idealism. I can't stand the idea of a world where natural laws stop being laws for us all, and it seems ridiculous that Marcia or anyone else could transform the laws of physics to suit their own ends, simply because the fantastic appeals to them."

"What's more likely," continued Slim, "is that you and Marcia don't live in the same world. The world of a blind person is wholly different from that of a person with sight or even from that of a myopic who can only distinguish shapes without the help of glasses and so lives in some kind of a halfway world."

"Subjectivity again," sighed Bill. "The world is given to us and it's up to us to disentangle the meaning of reality, which has to be the same for us all."

"This planet, this ball of earth," said Slim, "is barely more than a backdrop before which we enact an infinite series of realities. Are you going to tell me that Stephen's daily reality has some point of correspondence with that of Onassis'? Or that reality for St. Francis of Assisi was the same as for Machiavelli?"

"Pure verbiage. Neither words nor personal attitudes can change the world or its essential reality."

Slim and Marcia had reached the Edwards' house in time for tea. Several consecutive days of heat and humidity had enervated them, leaving them ripe for acrimonious argument. At long last that afternoon the static air had finally begun to shift, but there remained considerable humidity and great cottony clouds that seemed to be bumping the Teix.

The breeze was fresher on the Edwards' terrace. Judy came out of the kitchen with a tray bearing tea and biscuits, and took the opportunity offered by the first pause in the conversation to launch into an interminable monologue, in Faulknerian style and in her characteristically insinuating tones through labyrinthine alleyways, to describe her trip to buy a new mattress in Palma the previous day.

The previous week a cigarette stub had set fire to the sheets at four in the afternoon, and the whole house filled with smoke before Bill realized that something was wrong.

"See?" Marcia muttered to Bill quietly, "you're not going to tell me that Sonny was responsible for that? There's no doubt it was a salamander."

Bill wasn't given the chance to answer. Judy had taken over the reins of the conversation once more and was describing the new supermarket that had just been opened on the outskirts of Palma. Her story was interrupted by the first drops of rain. Everyone looked up at the sky. A huge black cloud had formed without anyone noticing.

"What bad luck," Judy commented, "it'd be better if we went into the living room."

Bill had sat tight in a mood of introspection, gazing into his cup of tea. When the first drops fell on his bald pate his face lit up. Clearly something had come over him. He rose to his feet with a sudden burst of energy and helped Judy collect the cups. Then he went over to Marcia, smiling.

"I'll give you proof of the fallacy of your ideas."

They all went into the living room except for Judy, who had an obsession for washing up the dishes the minute they had been used.

"Just a moment, please," Bill excused himself and disappeared into his study. On his return a few minutes later he was carrying a notebook. "Through some strange coincidence . . ."

"There is no such thing as coincidence," Marcia interrupted him.

"Please," Bill continued with a pained expression, "let me go on. Through some inexplicable accident, Ramón and Lucrecia brought me this book last week. It's an old Mallorcan book of spells they found in a derelict house above Sa Cova de ses Bruixes."

"Just a minute, please," said Marcia politely, "did they give you this before or after the bed caught fire?"

"Before." An uneasy silence fell.

"Sa Cova de ses Bruixes means the Witches' Cove, doesn't it?" asked Slim.

"Yes. It was an old smugglers' hideout. It seems entirely appropriate that a book of spells would be found near a place like that."

Heavy raindrops began to spatter the living-room windows and Bill heralded their arrival with a gesture.

"Ramón brought me the book so I could translate some of the Latin passages and explain the names of some of the demons he'd never heard of before. Now we have the perfect opportunity to verify the effects of all these texts against the forces of nature. Please pay attention." He opened the book and began reading from the top of a page: 'Prayer against lightning, hail, hurricanes and storms including those resulting from a curse.' Now you can see how badly it's written. Clearly Mallorcan witches are poorly acquainted with both Spanish and Latin."

And he began reading: '*Christus Rex, verut in pace et Deo Homo factus est verbum cara factum, Christus de Virgini pare, Christus crucifixus est, Christus sepultates est, Christus resurectis, Christus ascendit, Christus imperat, Christus reguat, Christus cumini fulgore nos defendet. Deus nobis cuem est.'*

As he finished, the storm increased. It seemed as though someone were throwing buckets of water at the windows. Marcia could make out indistinct shapes of trees bent double in the wind and a shiver ran up her spine.

Bill laconically went over to the window and continued:

'I invoke you, storm, in the name of the great and living God, and of Adonai Elosini, Teobach and Metrator, that you dissolve like salt in water and retreat to the uninhabited forests and uncultivated lands, causing neither harm nor damage.'

He solemnly made the sign of the cross to all four cardinal points.

'I repeat I invoke you by the four words that God Himself uttered to Moses, Uriel, Secaph, Losofa, Blat and Agle.' Here Bill paused to cough — "No doubt you will already have realized, because of the similarity of these names to those of the supernatural entities, that this spell derives from the Key of Solomon."

"I'd no idea," rejoined Slim.

"Bill," Marcia's voice sounded nervous, "once you've begun a spell it's terrible to interrupt the formula."

"Bah!" said Bill. "The storm's going on just the same, but I'll finish anyway."

He resumed his solemn tones and went on:

"'I entreat you to dissipate this moment, in the name of Adonai, Jesus Cuitem, Jesus Superamtem, Jesus Our Father even unto temptation; Legrot and Alphomiedes and Urat and

Conion and Lancaroa and Fondon and Arpagon and Atanat and Boragais and Serabeui.'"

He gave particular emphasis to the names towards the end of his recital and, when he reached the final "and Boragais and Serabeui," the world suddenly turned a livid blue, a vast explosion shook the house and all the lights went out.

"Very effective," Slim was laughing.

From the depths of the shapeless form of the sofa floated Marcia's distant voice: "Well, you brought it on yourself, Bill. Shall we light candles?"

Slim, who had spent the past seven years bogged down in chapter three of the definitive novel on Deyá, came down from his study in a good mood. He had produced a page and a half of crystalline prose and was certain he'd overcome his writer's block.

"What shall we do today?" he asked Marcia.

"We ought to go and say goodbye to June. Tomorrow she's leaving to spend three months in the United States."

"What do you say we stop off at Stephen's place and look in on the philosophers' stone? It's on our way."

"I don't know, Slim." Marcia sounded unenthusiastic. "He's bound to trap us there for goodness knows how long, while he goes into all his tortuous theories of which I understand nothing."

Slim got his way as usual. They found Stephen cheerful, jotting mathematical formulas down in his black notebook and consulting his pocket calculator from time to time.

"Hello, I'm pleased you've come. I've spent the last three days with this marvelous toy. Sit down and I'll explain it all to you."

The cage was hanging from a beam over the table. At regular intervals along the beam were nailed pieces of string with screws attached to the ends. Slim looked at them in surprise. Only the ones furthest away hung vertically from the ceiling. The rest were clearly drawn towards the cage.

"It is a black hole," Stephen confirmed, overjoyed. "I've been measuring the diameter of the accretion disc and the results are extraordinary, absolutely extraordinary. As you know, the force of gravity diminishes with the square of the distance so that, by ascertaining the weight of the screws and measuring their gravitational pull towards the black hole at various distances from the center, it's a simple matter to calculate the mass of the black hole. Do you know something, Slim?" Stephen was leaning towards him, "I calculate that there must be at least three hundred thousand tons of compressed matter in the nothingness at the center of this hole."

"Stephen," Marcia interrupted, "how can there be three hundred thousand tons of anything in a birdcage?"

"Ah, this is where we find out how clever old Lulio really was. Do you see these opaque metal objects encrusted in each of the eight corners of the cage?"

Marcia took a careful look and nodded.

"These are magnets," Stephen explained. "Their electromagnetic field is far more powerful than the force of gravity. These eight tiny magnets equidistant from the center balance the electromagnetic force engendered by the hole's rotation. They sustain the mass in a state of immobilization at the precise center of the cage."

"If you say so." Marcia was still skeptical. "But if I were you I'd keep the cage hanging from something more substantial than a rusty nail and a copper wire."

At this point June Redgrave came in with a Deyá basket slung over her shoulder.

"What a dreadful day it's been," she rolled her eyes as she kissed Marcia on the cheek, "I've spent the entire time packing and tidying up."

"We stopped off here on our way to your place to say goodbye," Marcia told her.

"Sit down, sit down," interjected Stephen. "I'll make tea for everyone."

He went to the kitchen and began filling the kettle.

"I can't stay long, Stephen," June said, "I've still got a thousand things to do. I came to ask if you'd look after Dicky while I'm away. You know Magdalena, my neighbor who usually looks after him, well she's beginning to get too old and senile for it. She'd be bound to forget to feed him and give him water."

"Who's Dicky?" Stephen had to raise his voice over the sound of the running water.

"My canary," replied June taking a minute cage out of her basket. "He'll be very good company for you. The cage you've got hanging up here would be ideal for him," she added, taking the bird out in her hand.

"June, no!" Slim and Marcia exclaimed with one voice.

Stephen's horrified face appeared in the kitchen doorway. "Don't touch the cage!" he was screaming.

"You'll frighten my poor little bird," June sounded indignant. She opened the door of the cage, placed Dicky carefully inside, and he disappeared.

"Dicky!" she screamed. "Good God, what's happened? He's vanished!"

Stephen fell over a chair as he ran towards the table and shut the cage door with a teaspoon.

"What have you done with my Dicky?" whimpered June.

"Nobody move," Stephen ordered severely.

He inserted the teaspoon between the bars and wiggled it back and forth, an expression of horror on his face.

"It's got out!" he exclaimed, "the black hole has escaped!"

"Where's my poor little Dicky?" wailed June with tears in her eyes.

"The black hole has swallowed him," said Slim.

"Everyone over here," Stephen ordered, "it must be somewhere on the other side of the room."

"What are you saying?" squealed June. "I want you to give my canary back."

Stephen took a copy of the London *Observer* out of the kindling basket by the chimney. "Here, Slim," he said. "Grab this and open it up. We have to track the thing down."

He opened a few of the pages and hung them over the poker. He looked like a toreador cloaking his sword with his cape. Cautiously, he advanced towards the cage, shaking the paper out in front of him.

"Grab hold of a broom," he told Slim, "we've got to find it and get it back into the cage. It will burn holes through the paper and we'll be able to tell where it is."

"You're madder than March hares," said June, "I'm leaving right now."

Stephen held out an arm to block her way and the two froze at the sound of a "ping-g" from the front door. A round hole appeared in its upper pane of glass.

"It's out in the street," said Stephen. "Time!" He was banging the flat of his hand against his forehead, "We have to measure the time it takes."

He fiddled with the knobs on his quartz watch and set the stopwatch. Then he got up on the table and sighted from the center of the cage to the hole in the window pane.

"Its trajectory is virtually horizontal, but it has to describe a descending parabolic arch as the earth's gravity attracts it. It covered over twelve feet in less than a minute. Let's go, Slim."

"We need a ladder," said Slim, "it has to be at least nine feet above ground level." Stephen ran through to the kitchen to collect the stepladder.

"Marcia," he called. "Unhook the cage and bring it to me."

Slim gradually pushed the front door, opening it little by little. No more holes appeared. June gulped back her tears as she descended the three steps to the street. The tiny cage dangled empty from her hand.

Slim took a broom from the kitchen and went out the door. Standing on the stone porch he swept the broom in the air from side to side, then uttered a yelp of surprise as it was snatched from his hands and vanished.

"It's here," he pointed, as Stephen appeared with the ladder. "It just swallowed your broom."

Stephen ran down with the stepladder and opened it in the middle of the street. "Bring the newspaper and the poker," he ordered Slim before turning to Marcia. "And you, open the door of the cage and give it to me."

He mounted the steps and began agitating the newspaper over his head. There was a "plop" and a smoking hole appeared at the edge of the paper.

"I think we've got it," he said tersely as he gradually moved the paper back. Another "plop," and another smoking hole appeared. In a semicircular movement, Stephen placed the cage behind the newspaper to trap the black hole. He lost his balance and cage, newspaper and poker were snatched from his hands and vanished into thin air.

Slim ran to break Stephen's fall, and they sprawled on the ground. They gazed disconsolately at the stone wall of Brad Rising's house where the black hole was opening a tunnel the size of a man's fist.

"It's beaten us," said Stephen, as the two of them got up, dusting off their trousers. "The cage was our last hope."

Brad Rising was away on a trip, his house closed up indefinitely. They could only go out in back and wait for the black hole to reappear, opening a path through the rear wall, an event that occurred approximately three minutes later.

"It's gaining speed and beginning to drop." Stephen was observing its passage, chewing up the leaves and branches of an almond tree in the patio as it went. "I estimate that if it doesn't run into the protruding rockface, its trajectory will carry it to the other side of the stream before it goes to ground and starts eating its way towards the center of the planet."

The three of them returned to Stephen's house and began slowly sipping their cups of tea.

"You said a week, didn't you?" It was Slim who broke the silence.

Stephen sighed and nodded. Suddenly there was a dull rumble and the three of them were paralyzed with fear as the house shuddered under their feet. The black hole had collided with the rockface above the stream. It opened up a tunnel at a steep angle, fracturing the stratified stone and precipitating the Great Deyá Landslide. All evidence of the disappearance of the black hole into the earth's maw was submerged in tons of loose stone that thundered into the stream in an avalanche.

Slim, Stephen and Marcia walked to the edge of the landslide with an air of resignation and looked down to survey the catastrophe. Margarita stood on the road running up the side of the Clot, looking up in horror. Tomeu, Francisca, Jamie, the corpse-dresser and most of the village children were there beside her.

"And this is just the beginning, is it?" inquired Slim.

Stephen nodded without replying and the three of them set off for their respective homes as night fell.

Clearly Stephen's calculations had gone wrong. The world didn't end the following week.

"It was a random calculation," he said by way of evading blame. "After thinking it over carefully and revising my equations it seems to me that the accretion disc could perform like a helicopter's rotor blades. If that's the case, its trajectory to the earth's center could be considerably delayed. Even up to several years."

Meanwhile the residents of Deyá were happy with the prices the Germans were paying for their old houses, and new restaurants began to spring up. A bank was built with a luminous sign at least *this* wide, more food shops and even a small supermarket which opened up along with a drug store, more boutiques and — worst of all — a discotheque which resulted in Carl, the composer living opposite it, abandoning the village.

Robert's health started to fail. Deyá was populated with strange faces and he was infuriated by the construction of a hideous bottled water factory that ruined the look of the village, that and a new highway that ran above the covered stream and began to run down towards the Cala, where no doubt a large tourist hotel would soon be constructed.

Robert had previously called in frequently at Ca'n Blau. He would sing songs from the First World War and teach Marcia the names of the stars and how to pay obeisance to the new moon.

The more Deyá expanded, the less Robert went out. The magic was leaving God's village. He confined himself to his house and spoke less and less, growing impatient with the conversations taking place around him, and gazing at the others with absent eyes, only rising from his chair to go to bed.

Deyá was no longer what it had been. The prophets stopped arriving and the witches left. Lucia stopped producing her magic skin creams and her cure-all potions. Stephen no longer set the table for tea. Don Pedro began selling off the church's saints, replacing them with chalk statuettes, and the cemetery was so modernized it actually admitted Protestants.

One fine day Stephen packed his one and only suitcase and returned to England.

"That's the signal," Slim told Marcia. "The village is finished."

A few weeks later they decided to go back to live in Central America. After all, Marcia still had her *ceiba* tree there.